FISTICUFF OF THE
SOULS

Carpe diem!
Matilda Pinto

FISTICUFF OF THE
SOULS

The Deliverance

MATILDA PINTO

PARTRIDGE

To order additional copies of this book, contact
Partridge India
000 800 10062 62
orders.india@partridgepublishing.com

www.partridgepublishing.com/india

CONTENTS

DEDICATION

To the two women with enough chutzpah,
Who savoured life despite many odds;
To the unsung women of my country,
Who live and die without selfhood.

DISCLAIMER

You are likely to find resemblances between the characters in the tale and the folks next door. Let this not worry you as the intent is to celebrate the uniqueness that binds all of mankind.

Regardless of my claim, this book is a work of fiction. The names and characters in this book are fictitious while places and incidents are near facsimiles. If you do find a resemblance to the living or the dead the onus is on you to ignore it.

PROLOGUE

Once there lived a feline couple, Tabby and Chibby. They each had a story to tell. It wasn't a story about one of their kind. For Tabby, it was a tale about his mistress, Teru, who had died without premonition. Unusually, she had refused to move on until she had answers to why life had put her through the wringer.

If only death provided her with the clairvoyance needed to look through the hearts of those who mattered to her, besides granting her access to a past, she would have the ripostes she was looking for. If Tabby were privy to this spiritual experience, to additionally being endowed with an earthy philosophy and characteristic cat humour, it would surely enable him to champion her cause. His amazing perspective of human life, made him direct Teru who wished to avenge the wrongs she had suffered at the hands of her husband with, "Why would you want to flood him out of his grave, why don't you tickle him out instead?" We can only presume, answers found, Teru would move on to her destination like all mortals and Tabby would return to terra firma to join Chibby, his soul mate.

Chibby's tale is so unlike Tabby's. Awra, her mistress of ninety-four lives life to the hilt, and is sceptical about God and the life to come. Chibby and Tabby are seen discoursing the many possibilities, if, Awra were to die. Would that make her revisit life as Teru did? Would that constrain her to regret having harassed a conservative Brahmin by constantly having dropped fish in his well in her passion to breed them? Would she dodge the angelic escorts facilitating her journey from the here to the hereafter as did her counterpart? Or would she get into a punch-up with the preordained blueprint of her karmic journey? Silence drowns the answers.

Discernment failing, one returns to Teru and Awra, to pick up gleanings from their myriad encounters of life. If they battle it out to square accounts with the living, not precluding the ones who had gone before them, perchance they would merit *moksha*. If only, they could untangle the glitches ...

End

FOREWORD

Fisticuff of the Souls is a tale about two women, Teru and Awra. It commences with a statement in just two words, 'Teru died.' Just when you presume that you could be reading the last line of the last chapter, it recommences to tell us that she refuses to be disremembered or seen off.

Despite the absurdities of life and death, Teru wasn't quite prepared for what was on offer on the other side of the turf. And what follows, leaves her bamboozled.

The other woman, on the other hand, …

To the one we are the aroma that brings death; to the other, an aroma that brings life. And who's equal to such a task?

Corinthians 2:16

PART 1

Not Everyone Lives

Chapter 1

A LIFE IS LOST

I

The Requiem

Teru died.

A daughter looked at the clock. It was 5 p.m. on the fifth day of March, of the year 2013. The timing seemed orchestrated as there was no summons, howsoever remote. Neither were there any death throes. Just a brief after luncheon slumber, from which Teru fought to wake up, but didn't.

Teru died while her tabby of thirteen slept fitfully on the window sill, with half an eye on his mistress. He had seen it all. Try as he did, he couldn't stop it. He remained rooted to the scene with a stiff and puffed up tail and eyes, inflammatory red. His whiskers were seen whipping this way and that because of a psychic prompting beyond his discernment for having failed her. When he came out of his agonising inability to fight the unacceptable, he thought,

This is no way to go. Wait till Teru gets to the Pearly Gates, if there is one, and her Reverend will be made to swallow fire and brimstone.

Poor Tabby. He had been an agnostic all his life. He hadn't heard of the likes of the apostles who professed that death came like a thief to filch life, leaving behind no signs of pillage or resistance. Nor had he heard of Teru's mom, the feisty Natal *Bai*. She had come all the way from the nether world, on the eve of her daughter's passing away. In the dead of night, she had woken up a favourite grand-daughter of hers making her jump out of her skin. Her voice, dry as bone, she had said,

Agnessa, Agnessa, ootgo. Ootgo Agnessa.

She didn't tarry long enough for Agnes to ask her,

But why?

Tabby having a limited intuitive frequency had missed it all. It happened in the remote village of Kedumullur at Teru's maternal home district of Kodagu. When he did get to hear of it, in his inimitable style he whipped his whiskers over again and stated that this was no mumbo-jumbo. He had heard Teru recount of such a visitation from Aunt

Rose who seemingly had been in a great hurry. She had tenderly nudged her niece of two and thirty out of her slumber to get her to set out on her last journey. Enamoured by her bewitching smile, the niece almost slipped out of her skin, when a chill breeze hit her to the bones. She opened her eyes to realize what it was that she was about to do.

Aunty Rose, how could you …? Don't you see that I have three little children to raise and besides ... Get out of here and go fish for some old hag elsewhere and don't you dare come this way again, the niece had foamed.

So, she had resisted the invitation.

The following morning, the niece had heard the bells toll for a less than middle-aged nephew of Aunt Rose.

Ever since, the niece has had several out of body episodes, claimed Teru. If it had anything to do with Aunt Rose or not is something Teru had refused to vouch for. In one of those dream occurrences, the niece was said to have been among those countless number of sealed coffins laid out in neat rows on a vast field like the terracotta army of China. Only, the niece was locked out of hers and she was running around rows and rows of coffins, opening and shutting them in utter despair to find her own, for fear of being sucked in by the all engulfing space. She preferred company, even if it was an untenable companionship. Tabby wished to forget such episodes for Teru's sake.

The bells were heard dolefully tolling for Teru. Tabby didn't quite approve of her becoming the focal point of discussion the world over, something he was not accustomed to, having lived the life of a recluse. Her family tweeted tearfully. *Daijiworld* featured her in the obituary. A remote acquaintance from another continent called to condole and the local newspapers had a memorial announcing her demise.

Tabby saw Teru's spectral self, sitting atop of a chandelier, very much part of the funeral plans. Contrary to his expectations, Teru lapped up the attention with *joie de vivre*. What she loved most of all was the ride she was going to have in a hearse from a daughter's house to her spouse's. The hilly, scenic route from the coastal town of Mangalore to the lush green plantation in Kodagu. Teru thought wistfully, some 333 kilometers was going to add colour to her final journey. Tabby, not the one to be left behind, discretely slipped beneath the hearse. Teru saw him cosy up to her under the silken white drapes.

All along, Teru kept an eye on the convoy that accompanied her. She didn't quite trust the youngsters who didn't care enough if an old lady was alive or dead. She wanted to teach them a lesson or two before she was altogether gone. She had nearly sat up in her coffin to smite the one among the family who stopped the hearse halfway through; no, not to look for a rest room, but a wine shop where he could pick up a bottle or two of, ... you know what.

Oh, these men folk, rued Tabby, not forgetting to tap the bottom of the coffin to comfort his agitated mistress.

It was to be a fair-weather funeral. But Teru was going to make them sweat it out before she called it a day. Closer to her destination, she had a huge tree uproot itself and lie supine across the road.

Good job Teru, whispered Tabby.

Eventually, they arrived at her destination and all and sundry exclaimed,

This is something to die for!

The house had transformed itself into a field of lilies. Amidst it was a customized crucifix with plump green peppers and ripe red coffee berries. All eyes were scanning the drapes and tapers, when Tabby nudged his mistress to ask,

Did you see that?

I didn't see any of this when I was alive and kicking! How does it matter now? she huffed.

Shush! You are too flustered for comfort, whispered Tabby.

And then came the Clunys from the convent next door with their 'Voice of an Angel' requiem hymns. This is something to lust after mumbled Teru humorously and tried to lip sync, but couldn't. With that she began to realize that the end was drawing near. Now it was the turn of the lay ministry and they chorused, each in a pitch of their choice. Teru nearly asked them to pipe down. That's when Tabby meowed to implore,

Lie still. He's here with the cruet in hand and dressed in a lacy alb.

Well, I don't mind if he can carry the notes. One other thing, tell me, is he fine- looking? she crooned.

Why do you ask? enquired Tabby with a tinge of suspicion in his voice.

My pictures you daffy … I don't want a fossilized, baldhead to officiate at my last rites. Oh, never mind, you'll not understand what it means to go in style, do you? said she miffed.

And then she shifted ever so slightly to her right to take a look at her offspring.

I was right all along, thought Tabby.

How could that one with rosy cheeks think of the post-funeral reception menu even before you have turned cold? he asked Teru.

The primogeniture, found comfort in the thought that he need no longer suffer from being tongue-tied during his rare and reluctant visits to his mother. The ones who had secured Teru's valuables wished to keep the deal under wraps and asked her to intercede for them to keep it so. The rest were not quite sure whether it was a good thing or a bad thing for her to have gone. Among them was the one who was trying to squeeze out a tear or two for the benefit of an audience that would talk of it for a while to come. Teru was disappointed to say the least. And the leave taking, seemed well rehearsed. How tenderly they sealed a kiss each on her cheek, appearing heartbroken and truly bereaved.

On the other hand, the village that had flocked to see Teru go, had a reason for being there. Babu had come to thank Teru for sheltering her on her loft when her father had come after her with a pestle in hand to pound the brains out of her skull, all for having eloped with a man she chose to marry.

The second, limped his way to the funeral home remembering the day Teru had saved his wife from being driven out of the village by a kangaroo court for being with child soon after their betrothal. She had nursed her back to health, risking her own safety at the hands of a husband not inclined to charity.

The one next to him paid his respect to Teru, the young bride of yesteryears, who took on a man's job of holding the plough-share to bring food to the table.

Teru's neck was progressively getting stiff. Time was slipping out. If only she could find a distraction, she thought. She could then put off the inevitable for some time and go smiling, when down came a cold drizzle.

A prodigal sprinkle of holy water, if you please, mumbled Tabby who didn't like to get his coat wet especially before the final act.

Teru wanted to return favour for favour by shaking the droplets off her remains like a drenched dog drying his pelt, but Tabby who didn't like dogs around him, not even a mention of them, pleaded,

Oh no, not now.

At St. Antonys, a structure that seemed to rise out of the verdant womb of the earth, Teru wasn't sure how to go about the service. Was she expected to listen to the homily or lie still? She tried tapping her feet when the choir assonated a chime that sounded like a thousand cowbells let loose all at once. Luckily, no one noticed Teru's attempt to keep beat as her remains were covered from head to toe with gaudy marigolds and chrysanthemums and clusters of rambling roses, freshly wrenched from the gardens, just short of uprooting the plants. They out did the lilies in their glazed paper and silken bows.

What a shame, thought Teru's kith, *the village folks have no taste.*

In a while, it was going to be curtain call for Teru. Her limbs were getting ramrod-stiff, and she didn't enjoy the sensation. She thought it best to distance herself from it all and join Tabby to watch the dust-to-dust act, seated on a tree top.

Nothing can be more harrowing than attending your own funeral, she told Tabby pensively.

There they go, trying to pick me up as if I were a sack of potatoes in a hurry to be dispensed with, she said to no one.

Six strapping young men, grandsons all and the two Johns. Watch me in action, said Teru.

Tabby didn't know what to expect. Teru was determined not to let the young men have it easy. As they walked the mile to the burial place carrying the coffin on their shoulders, she gradually doubled her weight and then she began to raise it to four times that number. Not done yet, she began to throw all her weight to one side which made the pall-bearers on that side fear a topple down. The boys began to buckle under the strain, but were not willing to concede defeat and ask for help. Two of them switched positions to balance the scale. Though not a math wizard, Teru saw their move and quickly shifted her burden to the other side and heard them say,

Oh boy, what's up?

Tabby was tickled at the sight of them.

Watch out Tabby, she said and began to rattle the floorboard.

The boys wondered if the coffin was going to come apart under her weight. Had the mortician remembered to nail the floorboard and tighten the screws? Panic gripped them. They nearly asked,

What if …?

By that time, they had lowered her on to the loose mound of fresh soil, on the slope next to her resting place. They looked thoroughly beaten by an otherwise, 'little woman,' who weighed no more than a few pearly grains.

After Teru's remains were interred, Tabby heard the tallest of Teru's grandsons tell his mother,

Seriously Mother, you better consider shedding some of that mass. Whoever expected granny to weigh so much? If that doesn't happen, I'm warning you Mom, there's no way I'm going to be your pall-bearer. I'll simply put you in a wheel barrow and tip you into the grave.

That's going to be fun. Teru make sure to be around when that happens. It'll be a scene worth watching, chuckled Tabby.

II

The Reverend

It didn't seem like a funeral house as everyone was enthusiastic about meeting everyone else and catching up on who was who at Teru's funeral. And Teru didn't want to miss any of it in death as in life. She was home before the rest. She had perched herself on the silken drapes of a settee from where she could see everyone and everything. She saw the male species huddled together on the porch to the sound of clinking glasses and the thrumming crickets.

Turn off the lights, they said, as pop went the sodas.

What a way to drown their grief, whispered Tabby from behind the drapes.

Wait till you see the mourner's meal, will you? Don't tell me it is the same old rice and *saambaar*, for all the times I painstakingly put out the steamed rice noodles with chicken stew, the pork curry with rice dumplings on the table ... for all the ..., lamented Teru.

Teru would have loved to smell just for one last time, the customary shrimp chutney and the sweet lime pickle, accompanying the *kanji* at funeral meals.

Just as well, thought Tabby.

For Teru's sake, he didn't want her heir apparent to shed crocodile tears when passing the bowl of brown-rice *kanji* among the mourners who partook of it as a mark of their solidarity in grief, as was done for ever so long among Teru's folks.

When grace was said and the meal done, the house gradually fell silent. Retiring to bed, one of them spotted a palm-sized moth on the settee. To Tabby's surprise, he clicked picture after picture of the nocturnal visitor and posted it on FB.

The rest, what were they thinking when they waxed eloquent, describing the chiaroscuro design on the wing? They went so far as to say, that it resembled their Mom's funeral sari. An overstatement, smirked **Tabby**.

The cacophony took Tabby's mind off Teru just a wee bit. When he next looked in her direction, she wasn't there. Disgruntled, he slipped out of his hiding and hopped onto the window sill of the dining room for a breath of fresh air. That's when he found himself staring into an old mirror with rusty frames, nailed to the wall. It was weird to think that he didn't find himself in the frame, but Teru who was beyond reach. Upset, he muttered,

Now, what next?

Tabby saw her enter a tunnel. Like the one, at Engelberg leading to Hotel Terrace. The Reverend with a hoary beard was awaiting her at the terminus with a far from readable face. From one of the two gothic windows behind him, Tabby saw a familiar high-cheeked countenance, bleached with anxiety, from having awaited heavens just verdict for over a decade. From the other, he saw no less than a dozen hands clutching the bars, peering at Teru with a welcome gaze. They were Teru's audience, connected by blood and experience, he presumed. The Reverend gesticulated and said that inside was an inviolate Coliseum which would play-out earthly doings.

Here you don't have to depose or plead before the sitting judge. Your *karmic* scores and the verdict play themselves out, said the Reverend.

And Teru being Teru, she was hell bent on having upright justice, no more, no less. It concerned her and not what the Reverend or the man cowering behind him thought. Nothing could bring her peace but fairmindedness by which she had lived.

Tabby was certain that the Reverend had heard her sarcastic mumble,

Quite the way it is done on earth, quite 'as in heaven,' indeed.

The Reverend having turned around to insert the key to open the door to the Coliseum asked Teru,

Did you say something?

There was no response, but a stinging twist of the sagging flesh on his aged bottom. Rubbing down his sore bottom he did a sharp round about to admonish her,

What was that for?

To his astonishment, he saw Teru halfway down the tunnel which was now full of amplified echoes. Through the ripples, he heard her agonised whining,

Innviolatte Colisssseum, my fooottt! I'll nott lett thingggss pplayy themmsselvess ouuuut, Oppenn my wouuundddss, nooo. Ittt can'ttt beee onnne sideddeddd as ittt wasss ddownnn therre. Petitionnn I'll ttill hee cconnfesssess lliabilllityyy to gguiilltt, ...liabilllityyy to gguiilltt, ... guiiltt, guiilltt.

Wwhenn I was thraasshed, thraasshed, my baby inside turrnned bluuu.
Wwherre was the Colisssseum thenn?

In olld age hounnddedd for dowry, ddiddn't itt resoooouuunnnddd inn heavvven?
I waaaass cheateddd, cheated, chea… out of a living in oooolllddd aaagge, yeeess, I waaass! The bonyy mann, he didd. Turnnedd mee a ddepenndentt!

Ddisspplaccedd I wwaass, yess, yess, havviinng a homme I haadd nonne.
Paaassseddd around I waaass like a diiissscaaardeddd raaagg from house to house, I waaass, by chiiillldrenn, my oooown.

Plleeaadd I'll. Plleeaadd I'll, plleeaadd, … plleeaadd, ...plee
Plleeaadd I'll.

Reeplaayy, I nooo waaanntt, I waaanntt it fairrr and sqquarrre,
Mesurre forr measurre. Youuuu readdyyy, I commm backkkk, noo readyyy I hovvverrr abbbouuut, noo troubbble.

I've a souuull I reckoonn wiitth, noo less, noo moore. Jusssttt fairr, be fairr, noo lesss, noo moore. Colisssseum, noo, apppeal for justice, I'll.

The menacing echoes gave the Reverend a headache he had never known before, forcing him to retire. At the other end of the tunnel, Tabby went deaf from the intimidating uproar. He decided to pay a visit to the tranquil cemetery for relief instead.

So, Teru is back, he thought relieved.

Tabby noticed that Teru was lost in making rills on the slope of the cemetery, multiples of them, all leading to the grave of her husband who lay next to her. Consumed with curiosity, he moved closer only to catch a spurt of dirt in the eyes, which she had sent flying with a twig, her shovel.

What is that in aid of? he asked rubbing his eyes sore.

Downcast, she mumbled,

All roads lead to Rome.

Tabby was no history buff and didn't have the remotest idea as to Teru's intent. He looked at her quizzically. In a while, he heard her say,

Soon it would be wet weather, these rills will carry the monsoon in there. I'll have him flushed out of his resting place and have him hover about between two worlds, you'll see, she bellowed vengefully.

Tabby didn't approve of her feat of engineering. He didn't like to get his paws wet, and a deluge he had no stomach for. With his cat-sharp humour, he told her that she could tickle him out of the grave instead, couldn't she? Amused, he watched her burrow a hole, all of six feet under, and soon heard the chaotic rattle of bones to the accompaniment of a helpless chuckle,

Hee-haw, hee-haw, from within.

The deceased was in no position to gather his loose skeletal remains to slip out of his 6'x3' hole. The twosome, Teru and Tabby began to twitter and then ended up in a convulsive roar of laughter at the old man's plight.

Teru decided to call it a day and get back to the old man whenever she chose to fix him. Teru mused,

This will be his Coliseum, here and under, his earthly deeds will be played out on a full screen, no imploring, and no pleading. As in heaven, so on earth!

And the Reverend who was a witness to Teru's lopsided sense of justice dreaded the day she would turn up at his gate with the earthly remnants of her bony husband in leash with evidence and witnesses trailing.

What will the fallout be like? A requiem doesn't sit easy with neither the dead nor the one dispensing judgment, the Reverend deliberated smarting from the sting on his bottom?

Chapter 2

LIFE OUTS YOU

I

Life Beckons

Teru lives.

Isn't that what Tabby said, coming out of his despondency? She has crossed over, one would have thought, but not altogether. Who better than Tabby to affirm this sentiment having put down roots in Teru's matrimonial home, *'Mi Casa'*, so named by a missionary? No one objected to his new found residential status, as in this part of the country a stray feline is welcomed as an auspicious omen auguring a betrothal or the arrival of a baby.

Tabby's relocation coincided with the onset of the cold and ruthless monsoons. Consequently, for months on end Tabby found himself spending time seated on the kitchen counter, resembling a ball of *pashmina*. The crackling warmth coming from the fireplace added to his creature comfort. So too, the molten glow on the soot-covered walls cast by burning logs. Occasionally, he would squint open his right eye and strain his neck to peer into the bubbling earthen pot on the fire place to take in the aroma.

Tabby would watch the lady of the house dropping what looked like anchovies into the red-hot gravy by handfuls, heavily seasoned with *kadi-patta*. And then he would hold his breath. He had discovered that in preparation for the ritual, the same minnows had been lulled with a salt wash to make them shed their slimy defence and their bowel content. But the kosher cleaning had not been potent enough to snuff out their life. Consequently, he saw them darting out of the pot, only to reluctantly land back in the sulphuric gravy, with a stiff plop. How he wished Teru was around to serve him steaming brown rice topped with a little of that spicy fish curry, his favourite meal of all.

Having shooed Tabby down the counter, the younger mistress of the house settled down to tap rice *rotis* on a damp cloth. Her fingers refused to move with the dexterity Teru had effortlessly displayed *roti* after *roti*. She reminded him of the neighbourhood potter back home at Kodial who had a similar touch. He had marvelled at the way the soft dough yielded to Teru's nimble touch with the end-result of an 'O' of a *roti*. The pan-roasted 'O' soon puffed like the full moon when Teru reclined it against a pile of molten cinders. But her counterpart was disappointing with her *rotis*, uneven in thickness and jagged edges. Reconciled to a life without Teru's culinary expertise, he decided to settle for just the fish and give the *roti* a miss.

Tabby, then stole a catnap. On waking up, he couldn't think straight. The household was done with the meal and his bowl held a cold portion of fish and *roti*. One mouthful of it and he vaguely remembered having had a friendly tussle with Teru over his growing attachment to her spot near the fire place. Weary from the nocturnal squabble, he stretched himself full length and looked around for a seat to nestle in and then he saw her. Teru, on the murky manual stone grinder which was as old if not older than she. She was dripping pitter-patter and seemed at home with the puddle around the cold stone. In that state, he showed no inclination to snuggle into her dank lap for a snooze.

Teru waited for a while to get his attention and then began her saga.

Look, will you? said she pointing to the fields.

Tabby remained indifferent, but she continued all the same.

I had been to wade in the terraced fields for old times' sake, she fondly reminisced.

Now that she was free from worldly trappings, Teru wanted to experience first-hand, that tug, which compelled her little daughter and her siblings to sprint to the inundated fields of paddy on a rainy day. To splash around. Of course, Teru was chagrined. She never forgave them for the piles of clothes she had to stone wash soon after. The eight naked brats were then ducked in hot water before tucking them into bed with a piece of her mind. Resenting aqueous stories, Tabby continued to ignore her.

As in the days of old, Teru had opened the dykes so that the fish had the right of passage to course along the gushing waters. Through the myriad fields down the terraced slope. Churned by the rain fed waters, the fish then landed in the U-shaped sturdy cane basket pegged at the fall.

I bent low into the basket to get hold of a handful of those evasive but succulent creatures, just for you Tabby when ..., said Teru tilting her wrists left to right and then from right to left to draw attention to her empty hands.

She had slipped into the basket headlong. It was with a near gargantuan effort that she had fought the bundling waters beating her down. Getting out of the basket which was deep enough to drown an average man had seemed a lost game at that time of the night. And indeed, Teru was now pint-sized. Tabby was moved to tears and even crooned a meow-melody for her thoughtfulness.

Wait till you hear more, she said with a conspiratorial tone.

II

Finding the Unhallowed

I saw him with his band of cronies paddle waist-deep in the surging waters, Teru resumed her yarn.

Who ...? Tabby asked with a creased forehead.

With a toothy grin, she replied,

Who, but the Reverend and I gave him the slip.

Tabby had heard it said that the wandering dead provoke cosmic hubbub at the purgatorial cusp between the living and the dead. He asked himself,

What if the all-embracing forces were after Teru to escort her to where she belonged?

He chose to shrug off these eerie thoughts. And as a favour to Teru, Tabby came out to the veranda and jumped onto the *aimara*, a mud-caked parapet with a polished timber-top. On it stood the carved rosewood poles supporting the stoop, and he craned his neck to catch a glimpse of the hallowed entourage. In its place, he saw that the deluge was receding and the emerald crown of the paddy nurslings had been mowed down by the coursing waters which had raced over their heads. And the Reverend was nowhere to be seen.

In his stead, the following day, Tabby saw Armugan in the field. With a whip in hand and not a stitch on his body, this man with his flapping shame, was running after a pair of rebellious bullocks. They were bolting away with the plough-share in their track, leaving behind serpentine furrows they had marked ever so slowly and laboriously. Under the lashing rains, and on empty stomachs too. They were not going to have this naked man with only a thread across his chest twist their tails. His yoke fellows in the adjacent fields looked on from the corner of their eyes and tucking the tips of their thumb and index fingers into their mouths, whistled, 'Here, here'. Thus, jeering a man whose windblown loin cloth was flying abreast of him like a reluctant kite. They were seen slightly nudging their oxen pairs on their flanks with the command to continue their furrowed march through the slushy fields,

Hara, hara Shambu, Ramu *hara, hara.*

Get off that grinder and pat yourself dry at the fireplace, will you? Tabby exhorted the still drenched Teru to hide his embarrassment.

And she obliged, but not before reckoning with experiences that were played out in the presence of a mute witness all that while ago. The grinding stone!

III

Innocence versus Experience

Those many years ago, the ill-disposed neighbour had taken over the night with his hoots, accompanied by the discordant orchestra of crickets. Teru's terrified children had flocked around her for sanctuary. To the rhythm of the turning stone abrading the fragrant spices, Teru had rolled out story after story to soothe their panicky minds.

It was here that they learnt of the mythical Sita. They walked with her into the thick woods consumed with a sense of abandonment. They tearfully vowed to stand by Sita and rock her baby. The youngest of them all, choking on her emotions asked,

Mama, I'm very sad, are you too Mama?

Likewise, they had also learnt of the burglar who broke into a poor household, but had forgotten his job at the aromatic scent of the *moong dhal payasam,* which tingled his nostrils that he sat down to savour it. He guzzled it to the last mouthful. Salivating for more, he got his head into the pot to lick bottoms up. Oops!

The pot proved to be his booby trap. Unable to extricate his head from it, he ended up on a blind run while being thrashed black and blue by a grandma with a worn-out broom. Regaled, all but one of Teru's children curled into tight balls quite like pill bugs and rolled on the ground brimming with joy at justice breaking the back of a rogue. But the sad one, she fearfully looked out of the window for signs of a lurking burglar.

As good a story teller that Teru was, conversely numbers were her nightmare. She hadn't much of an education. Her seven-year old came to her rescue and taught the older and those after him how to unscramble the millions from the zillions so to say, all under Teru's watchful supervision. But when it came to her God and His tenets, she stood her ground like the formidable grinding stone. She painted for them a heaven so delightful, that they took off on wings of fancy to meet their Maker and tread a measure with the cherubs. On the other hand, the stories of a disobedient Lucifer roasting brown on ruddy coals and smoking through all the orifices made them cringe with fear and they pledged to keep away from the vile ways of the world. His disparate cries for water to quench his thirst fell on deaf ears, which Teru so mimicked, that it petrified the children. Nevertheless, there were times when they gave into temptation without fear of consequences.

Teru seated motionless on the grinding stone, was cagey about snapping her ties with life and was disconsolately nostalgic for the sunny old times she had had raising her children. Holding back tears, she turned to the loft and pointed to a 3'x3' vent from which hung a bunch of tightly-packed yellow bananas within reach of an adult.

My eight hungry mouths came up with ingenious ways of getting to the bunch, she said to Tabby with a cadaver chuckle.

Teru recounted the instance. A boy from her brood instead of getting to the bunch from below, had gotten over it from the attic and had bent a notch too low to plunder the forbidden fruit. Rather than climbing a stool piled on another stool, as is normally done. He missed his footing for a second time and landed in a copper pot filled to the neck with rice. The commotion got Teru to the scene resulting in a sound thrashing of the banana *chor* for having failed to honour the tenets of a large family which is, shared anything tastes like manna.

Teru would have spared the *chor* the ignominy had she known that this boy of hers had narrowly escaped from the jaws of death only a moon away. Teru heavy with her last child had managed to steal a siesta that noon. The seven trouble shooters took advantage of her heaviness and slipped out of the house looking for adventure. The banana *chor* made it his mission to scale a lofty wild-jack tree that afternoon to entertain his siblings. It had a sprawling wing-span laden with spiky fruits. He capered along the length and the breadth of the tree to the admiration of those below. Intoxicated with his feat, he leaned a long way away to get to a dangling jack which played hide and seek with the westerly sun against his line of vision. He wrenched the jack from its fibrous stalk and soon discovered that he was all hands and no feet. He came hurtling down through the branches holding on to the jack as if it were an Olympian torch. He found himself crashing through space.

There are those who never learn, for such history repeats itself, Teru reflected.

The rest, being nearly as young or a little older, were unable to tell if the *chor* was alive or dead, for he lay there with not a whimper. Nothing said, they carried his sagging weight by his spread-eagled limbs and placed him on his bed. They took measures to keep all signs of the mishap under wraps. They barred his window and the door was heavily guarded. That way, intruders like Teru were kept away and his agony was confined to the room.

A disreputable lot, Tabby thought.

And Teru couldn't believe that they had managed to keep her in the dark for the length of her life time. All she remembered was the fact that the banana *chor* had developed an inexplicable stutter overnight, which made sense to her in her present state awaiting transformation.

At evening prayers, a headcount showed a broken order. Teru dredged up the episode and saw herself raising her eyebrows only to be told by the youngest,

Shoo Mama, it's a secret, you mustn't ask.

Another face-saver stepped into say that the missing one had grazed his knee which hurt a bit, that's all it was and the rest nodded. Such accidents being every day, Teru recalled having dismissed it. Further, at meal times, Teru saw them covertly smuggling scraps of food to the invalid which then went unnoticed, an act of kindness which was more of an exception than a rule for a household of the size and kind. The routine meal-time melee with fisticuffs and punch-ups were the order of the day. When two of them coveted the gizzard, or fought over the drumettes, Teru wondered if these siblings were out to debunk the theory of fraternity.

Amid it all, a faint smile of reminiscence glided on Teru's face at how her seven-year-old trying to fight sleep had rubbed his eyes with curried fingers resulting in a radioactive turbulence. Blame it on the fiery chicken stew. Teru had rescued him from the sting in the eye with a wash. Just as she ordered him to get into bed, the brute came awake and returned to the table to claim his portion of chicken left uneaten, only to discover that it had been gobbled up by his immediate neighbour No.4. in the descending order of roll call. The nasty tussle which followed had them scream bloody murder provoking the five farm dogs to bark all together.

In a big household, a bird, however generous, can only stretch so far to feed the countless mouths, reflected Teru. She at her wits end, had promised to place another bird on the table, the first thing in the morning. The uncompromising loser was not willing to settle for anything less than the same v-bone from the same fowl, that instant, as he had a wish to make, the nature of which none of the others had a clue to. A curious Teru, tried to get a peephole view of the event. She saw the older lot trying in vain to discompose him with their wild guesses:

So, you want Mama to deliver a baby sister, don't you?

He refused to bite the hook, and Tabby heard Teru giggle over the seven-year old's tenacity.

No? You want mama to have twins, do you? The two of them will have your v-bone out and pick your brains too, mark my word, said another of them.

Oh no. I think he wants Myra to sit next to him in class, right? teased a sister.

Their every attempt to placate him fell on deaf ears and there seemed to be no end in sight. He continued to whine,

Me want my chic ….

Eventually, he fell asleep over the missing piece, stated Teru.

Teru driven up the wall with their tantrums had focussed on getting through the ordeal before she could call it a day and bid them goodnight. Retrospection brought a smile to her frosty blue lips.

Nonetheless, the relentless one was full of promise, Teru observed.

Tabby had no quarrel with her on the issue as he was in awe of the way he had gone after the rabbit waiting to be skinned. The boy was playing around waiting for his mother to come out of her bath and tuck him into bed when he picked up a soft thud and followed the trail to stop the rabbit, a game catch, sliding off the dining table in a bid to escape. His father's air rifle had left a nick in the ear sending it into a stupor, but it wasn't enough to snuff the life out of him.

In another instance, he became the hunted, Teru continued. An abominable neighbour had planted *supari* killers, imported from the vicinal state of Kerala, to do away with the man of the house over an altercation on right of way. At six feet and months away from turning a teen, he was treading the mile at daybreak to pick up the *Deccan Herald* from an automobile that plied through the dense coffee plantation. He was accosted by a pair of beefy *mundu* clad men who emerged from behind the coffee shrubs. Baring their tobacco-stained teeth they were known to have asked,

Son, can you tell us where the Christian landlord's house is?

He then winked at his companion saying,

Something *Mi Gasa*, right brother?

Hardly did the teen open his mouth in response, he was knocked down by a stinging box on his left ear. Fear of the unknown had shaken him out of his morning inertness. He was seen rolling down the hill a couple of times before rising to bolt out of the place. He did a steeplechase across tracts of coffee trenches, a couple of barbed fences and a shallow stream. To his good fortune, from the hill diametrically opposite to the incline he was on, his father was setting out to take an early bus to attend court hearings. He saw the boy's head bobbing up and down among the misty green slopes only to hurtle down the hill. Close on his heels, he caught sight of the speeding men coming to an abrupt halt, to stand and stare at their setting prey. They were no match for a thoroughbred country lad. The next couple of days saw the arm of law combing through the plantations, but to no avail. Expectedly, the perpetrators had gone underground in God's own land.

Tabby wagged the tip of his tail ever so slightly in relief. In a far from reproachful tone, Teru asked Tabby,

Have you ever met a man who is grossly benevolent or for that matter downright baneful?

Not sure of what Teru was getting to, he shuffled through his data bank while she accessed a remote past to view the lives of those who mattered to her, a past which was now available to her. A play-back of sorts, so to say. Cracking her stiff knuckles, she acknowledged with regret that the relentless one, bright as he was, had a vile streak to him. Well concealed from the rest, including her.

Isn't that what made him pick up those dry nuggets of human faeces and wrap it in emerald green Parry chocolate wrappers? asked Teru.

Back at the boarding school after vacation, his sister stumbled upon the surprise in her school bag which appeared heedfully overdressed. All the same, she had opened it with a ravenous appetite, not uncommon in a boarder. And she was vexed to find that the trickster had gone off limits. How she wanted him lynched except that there was no way she could nail him down with evidence.

Look what the influence of the spirit and character of erotica does to the pubescent? Can you beat it? It's the same one who saw in his head a scene between his sister in her teens and their neighbour of the same age making out on the loft. The one above your head, where the nectarine sweet *raspoori* mangoes were laid out on a warm bed of straw for ripening, Teru pointed out to Tabby on a sombre note.

Watch how the story is making its round and how the unfortunate ones respond when it reaches them, said a horrified Teru.

They are thoroughly flummoxed by the abominable innuendo, continued she.

Tabby squirmed at the thought of it and said,

How could he, ...?

As the scene of the duo making a suicidal pact to jump into the well, if subjected to an inquisition passed before her eyes, Teru felt rigor mortis tingle her bones, and a freezing fear grip her soul.

I would have lost a loved one for no fault and earned a never-to-die-scandal to tarnish my family, she sighed.

In those times, there was no way children could stand up to their elders and speak on or convince anyone of their innocence on matters such as these. Not with Teru with her Victorian morality and least of all her gun wielding spouse with a stiff upper lip. But by evening, the scandal died a natural death given the lack of perseverance of the very young sensationalist.

What a breather, sighed Teru years later when there was hardly a breath left in her.

It came as a revelation to Teru that the victim was not unlike her brother. She found her expression in trying to suckle her year-old sibling. And in a family of that size, nothing escaped the scanner. All the same, there was no finger pointing, no confrontation, but a nickname ingeniously coined to nail the aberrant. She was simply called, 'Marsha,' for it happened beneath a tree, beside the marshes, where the kids had been to gather blue berries. Since then, a lot of water has flown under the bridge, but the name; it hangs around her neck like the albatross.

As adults, they no longer use it, but Teru saw it stored in the recesses of their souls.

Some memories die hard, they do, reflected a brooding Teru.

Of a sudden, Teru glowered in disbelief. Tabby looked about him to check if the Reverend had made his appearance. Finding no trace, he asked her,

Are you alright?

Not now, not ever, not after I have seen what I now see, she said grinding her teeth with rage.

The rosy cheeked one, she turns out to be the Magdella of the lot. Qualms she had none when she squandered her honour on the streets, she supplemented.

Incredibly carnal for someone so young, bemoaned Teru with embarrassment.

Teru's deepest regret was in not having stopped her from sullying the marital home of her sister. Teru's filial impulse had blinded her then and as an earthling she had refused to believe the wagging tongues. But death is a strange bedfellow and here she was in a time warp where the doings of her progeny were staring her in the face. All she did was stare back in the consolation that the burden of another's misdemeanours would end the day death claimed her in its entirety.

It was not the end of Teru's flagellation. She saw yet another of her offspring being drawn to her own kind in the boarding house. But to her heart's ease, she saw her snap out of it as quickly, but not without retribution for the aberration. The mother in Teru got a keyhole glimpse of her daughter who was a stranger to her own marriage bed. It followed that with discernment, her pangs would pass and her rejection by her spouse would cease to matter.

Teru then saw the disconcerted father of her children, making his appearance. Teru looked askance and denounced him,

A disgrace, and perish such pernicious acts!

Teru saw him eyeing Nebisha's full lactating breasts through her threadbare *kuppayam*, much to the woman's chagrin. The poor woman's scanty headscarf didn't quite hide her modesty. But when it came to Mahadevi, the Malayali, she seemed to be making a statement with her figure hugging blouse which barely covered her assets. Besides, her mid-riff was exposed. To Teru's embarrassment, her *mundu*, a seamless length of cloth, which went around her from waist to the ankle, accentuated her contours, determining everyman's fall. She walked like a sculpted dancer from the temples, balancing the polished brass pots filled to the rim, one each on her head and waist. The water brimming over, bathed her face and drenched her torso, making her ever so seductive. He didn't resist her and she reciprocated. Her *thorth*, which, instead of cloaking her bosom, had been twisted to fashion a ring to rest the pot on her crown. All along, Teru had dismissed the scandals as gossip. If only she could stop the scene from unfolding.

As an afterthought, she asked herself,

Is this what the Reverend meant, when he said, life as lived would be played out at the Coliseum? I dodged the Coliseum to only have it come after me.

Teru wanted a debate with Tabby. But he had dozed off wary of human contradictions. He had kept asking,

How could man evolve codes for self-governance and then merrily flout them soon after?

The intrigues of mankind were something he couldn't digest. He was happy being the cat that he was with no moral compulsions to circumvent. Like Tabby, Teru too was agitated at first at the ambiguity of it all, but subsequently conceded that deliverance in the hereafter was so unlike that on earth. For better or for worse, she would be her own judge and was at liberty to choose her verdict, her just dessert, no less, no more. All the same, she was up to her nose to find out how much the husband's portion of penitence weighed. Only to realize that the curiosity of the kind was of no gravity, not in death. She reluctantly let go of her contention as the knowledge that was denied to her in life was now available for the asking.

IV

Ordained Encounters

Unmindful of the drizzle, Teru got off the grinder and took off in the direction of the cemetery, leaving Tabby to his feline dreams. She wanted to check if the recent deluge had flushed her, 'till death do us asunder companion', out of his gloomy hole.

A weird sense of comic relief, chuckled Tabby later.

To Teru's disappointment, everything appeared as was, in fact, fresher being rain washed. Nature stood out consummately at peace with herself. Browbeaten to give up the turmoil within her soul, she read the writing on her headstone,

See. I told you,
You die before you have lived.
29.9.1929- 13.3 2013

The epitaph far from composed her ruffled nerves. Fixing her gaze on the overhanging bank of clouds, she was torn between wanting to get into her fresh grave to keep away from the anytime torrential downpour and a return to the funeral home. Undecided, she took shelter under a tree. In the stillness of the evening, so familiar to the dead, she sensed that she was being watched. She was annoyed to discover that not one but several pairs of unreadable eyes were peering down at her from among the branches. She chose to ignore them, but not for long. She heard them whisper,

It is her, it is Teru.

What were they so cheery about? Teru wished to enquire.

Bracing herself to give them the slip, Teru took one last look at them. Their infringement on her private moments of reckoning with life and death had stupefied her. There he was, the familiar golden-ager, her father-in-law. He wore that self-same chequered head scarf bunched at the nape of his neck like a tail. Over it, he had his characteristic top hat with the hard brim, the indistinguishable brown muffler around his neck with one end coming down his left shoulder over that grey woolly cardigan, all the worse for wear. There was no mistaking that it was him as the cardigan had identical jumbo cable knits in three vertical rows, one in the centre, and two others aligned to the left and right side of his chest. He still had the warm flannel binding running along in circles from his ankles to the knees, ending where the pair of khaki short pants nearly kissed them. And those gumboots completed the picture. This was the man she had looked up to, but had never met except in that portrait hanging on the wall over the threshold of her house.

The exemplar, the patriarch of the family, her father-in-law. Why the appearance now? she was curious to figure out.

Teru had a total recall of that night in the early years of her marriage. She couldn't wait to share it with Tabby. The night had everything to do with the man with the muffler. Hardly had she retired to bed on one of those two rosewood beds, with her spouse snoring in the other, when a dream took hold of her. She saw the exemplar, leading Maidu's dozen buffaloes to her *Chingiri Ari* field, heavy with the delicate aromatic sheaves of ripe paddy. The fat ones ate the corn endlessly while Teru tossed and turned in bed. Her struggle to come out of her slumber, to hurl a baton at the elder for not caring enough to protect his household came to naught. After what seemed like an overwhelming devastation, she broke into a sweat and out of sheer exhaustion rolled over to her side and it worked.

Teru was awake and heard the dogs on the estate barking relentlessly. But her husband was lost to sleep. To wake him up, she sat at the edge of her bed and cleared her throat, opened the 2'x4' window to let in the cold breeze to tingle his bronchi ravaged nose. She then flung a shoe at the low ceiling to create a thud that could easily wake up the dead and tried tugging at his sheet a little at a time to bring him out of his post orgasmic sleep.

Tabby would have wanted to know as to why Teru didn't get him out of bed by hollering out his name or splashing a bucket of cold water over his sleepy head. Well, how was he to know that Teru for all her pluck could take no such liberty. She could go as far as getting his attention through an emissary or through a gesture and sound, but addressing him by his name was tantamount to impudence.

What is so sacrosanct about his name? Tabby may have added.

To cat mates, who fearlessly guarded their individual freedom, such subservience seemed nothing short of loathsome. Anyone who has watched the cats in action, in the thick of night, will vouch for their primal ruggedness in accepting or rejecting an offer. Finally, with closed eyes Teru heard him mutter more to himself,

The cock hasn't crowed yet, has it?

Teru took advantage of the rationalist's wakefulness to haltingly brief him on her dream.

He dismissed her with a,

Tut woman, tut, and curled up giving into another bout of sleep.

But the obstinate dogs being on Teru's side didn't let the husband sleep over her nightmare. He chucked his blanket to the foot end of the bed in a warm heap and peered into the darkness from the hole of a window. There they were, going hammer and tongs at nothing, bow, wow, bow wow. He decided to investigate. He strapped the headlight around his crown and loaded his air rifle and set out in the direction of the fields, downhill. Of course, he had the pack of dogs for reinforcement. They were gone for a while and Teru heard the dogs go berserk with their howling, but gun shots she heard none.

At last, when the sun was well on his uphill march, they returned. The rationalist appeared mollified. To Teru's relief, it turned out that the buffaloes were on their way to the field having discovered that the bamboo-pole barricade to the shed had slipped out of the loop. And only two of the ravenous bovines had managed to mouth a portion of the juicy aromatic sheaves of corn.

The dream, what was it all about then? Did the exemplar fast forward the scene to warn his household of impending perils? Or was it a pre-meditated act of warning to the earthlings of their duty towards their forerunners? Teru wished to ask someone.

Her father-in-law had bypassed his son, her husband for the clairvoyant act and deservingly so. Her husband had not remembered his precursors for over a decade. Teru just let him know that *Aan*, her father offered an annual prayer service and a feast to the poor in honour of the deceased members of the family.

So, ...? he seemed to ask with a raised eyebrow and nothing more said.

The exemplar and his band of celestial cronies were still watching her surreptitiously. And a thought crossed her mind,

Is the elder hand in gloves with the Reverend to entice me to follow his league and move on? Is it incumbent on the hovering souls to leave the terrestrial residents alone?

Teru pondered cocking her head to stare at the lot of them who appeared incommunicado. She wasn't ready yet to snap her umbilical connections with life. She edged away disregarding the seemingly benevolent presence of the lot of them.

V

Return to the Ark

Teru took the long route to the funeral home, wading through the choppy waters of the streams, lit up by flashes of lightening. Entering through the backdoor, she found her way to the smoky fire place in the bathroom and sat down before a smouldering fire for warmth. Half-dozing, she went back to another time and another way of life when this house was chock-full of life.

Teru looked at the strips of wild boar and farm raised pork, shriveled and dry, suspended on steel hooks over the fire place. Her household used it on a hard day when it was impossible to find any game. The mega ceramic jars on the loft, sealed and out of reach of children stood before her. Jars that had salted pork, cooked mangoes, Madras cucumbers and pickles that saw the family through the year when food was in short supply. Teru fondly remembered soaking the dry meat for hours on end to soften and desalt it. She had painstakingly cooked the lip smacking *pandi curry* in combo with big chunks of curry banana or yam on a slow fire, which was something to live for. She saw her husband, as if it were yesterday, approvingly licking his fingers of all trace of the viscid gravy and smacking his lips to take in the lingering taste. She always roasted the condiments before coarsely pounding it to give the preparation her signature stamp. Teru rebuffed anyone wishing to repeat the same with a smile and an equally evasive reply,

Very simple, add a little of this and a pinch of that. It can't go wrong.

It was patented, she would later gloat. So much so, the preparation died with Teru ending a chapter of culinary magnificence of her household.

Still in a daze, she visualized her corporal self walking a few steps and looking up the ladder leading to the loft. To see if her husband was anytime coming down having filled the fire-dried jar with the pickle for the fortnight. A menstruating or a lactating woman had no access to pickled sours in the jars. The bewildering memory of spiced fragrance not discriminating tingled her nostrils and she sneezed, *achoo*, and she heard a prompt, God bless.

Teru turned around and saw Tabby, and it dawned on her that the meat strips and pickles belonged to an irrevocable past to which she had no claim being at present in a state of limbo. She also realized that she was in good company, with a familiar frog and a hen.

Blotch the frog, a timeless relic of the house was the size of a civet's double pouch gland, grey and mouldy. He lived under the shiny copper pot used for storing drinking water in the kitchen. In Teru's lifetime of over half a century in that house as it's mistress, where nothing escaped her attention, she hadn't managed to see how he got under or out of the bottom of the pot which rested on a cane ring. In time for breakfast, the nine-year old Blotch would be there below the table to pick up scraps that the children dropped or to dart his tongue out to get the common houseflies for a meal. His favourite seat was on the feet of the master, who sat on a bench in the kitchen weighing his post- independent political options from the *Deccan Herald*. Occasionally, Blotch would be seen passing under his instep arch tickling the otherwise humourless man to a room full of hee haw, hee haw, to the surprise of all. Blotch wondered why the master had gone cackles when all he had done was pass under the Suez Canal.

Chingaari, the hen, on the other hand, favoured the womenfolk and she had a free run of the house. She was accustomed to jumping on to the *vakhil baank* to sit next to Teru and peck at the meters and meters of lace she had been crocheting. Seemingly, in her attempt to undo Teru's labour of love. One afternoon, she appeared jittery about something and she went cluck cluck cluck in Chicklish. Teru appeared to understand her every whim and remembered responding to her feathered complaints,

So, you have laid an egg for the day. Great job girl and thanks. ... Something bothering you? ... Your rooster goes gadding about with younger pullets? ... That's a shame. Just you wait. One of these days you will see me immerse him in hot water.

In a trice, Chingaari's rooster, the one with the gnarled neck presented himself before Teru. She had no idea as to what had caused the disfigurement to an otherwise statuesque neck. To her dismay, she saw the scene unfurl before her gradually: it had been a day full of expectations, a day in 1962 when Teru and her Gandhian husband had set off to town to cast their vote in favour of the incumbents to give Nehru another term as their Prime Minister. With no parental supervision, her bushy tailed children for want of anything better to do, went after this rooster to try their hands at pepper chicken. Having got hold of him, they were faced with a herculean task.

Who will wring his neck? they asked in chorus.

Not me, not me, not me ... replied each one in sequence.

In the end, a plot fell into place: in the pecking order, No.1. with her back to the sacrificial bird, stood over the rooster's legs to hold him down; No.2. exerted pressure on the wings which were clipped back together, keeping it close to the ground; No.3.

nailed down the winged creature by ramming his body with her hands and No.4. schemingly pressed the neck into the hands of the gullible No.6. to be turned around with a little help from No.5. The rooster's neck went around once, it went around twice, it went around one more time without as much as anyone flinching, not even the unsuspecting dandy. On the fourth round, everyone sensed the rooster's unwillingness to make a mockery of his sculpted neck. On the next move, they felt resistance course through every cell of his being and the seismic waves were felt rippling in all directions of their beings as well, not sparing even the least of them. One by one, they loosened their hold on the prisoner. No.6. certainly, didn't like the sensation that coursed through her little fingers and she let go of the neck and the rest brusquely followed suit and witnessed a proud neck unwind in slow motion. Though twisted out of shape, with painstaking deliberation the neck began to unwind itself- five, four, three, two and one. The rooster stood upright and still for a moment, unsure of the momentum he had recovered. As slowly, he began flapping his wings, convulsively at first, shedding a few of his coloured feathers and soon with an urgency as he became aware of the urge to escape from the presence of these monsters. With a dishevelled mane, he walked. Walked with the gait of a headless man in stupor. The notorious six aborted their culinary venture and scooted from the place with unsettling screams, in the company of a petrified cockerel.

A hapless Teru put out her hand to soothe the cockerel's nearly broken neck wishing to recant the disfigurement that had been caused by her own. She simply said,

I'm not the keeper of their conscience, even if they are my own.

In a subsequent scene, the same chanticleer had stuck his neck out on a pleasant evening. Teru's children were back from boarding schools. Every evening, they gathered in the backyard to feed some two hundred odd barnyard fowls. They were let out before the twilight hour for airing: the Minorca's, the slate-coloured guinea fowls with their white-spotted plumage, and the Syrians with their soft plucked necks. They came on their wings, overtaking the other for attention and space, from their three-tiered coop. Mushy husk mixed with diced vegetable, bran and kitchen waste was laid out for them in trough after trough. Whole grains of paddy were strewn around for those who preferred to peck and feed.

In the middle of it all sat the master's favourite daughter No.2. on a make-do stool fashioned from a tree stump. She was shining her star-shaped golden ear tops, mounted with a nacreous pearl each, with soap-nut suds. It's not given to the fowls to know the difference between fodder and bread. Therefore, the saying, *Kun'no khalear undeachi ruch-uch nam.*

A couple of roosters who otherwise kept their territorial distance from each other came together and stared at the brilliance and went cluck cluck clackety cluck. One of them gobbled the ear top and disappeared in the crowd. Only Holmes could have figured out which one of them had smuggled the jewel to woo his girl. He moved so fast among the pullets, the lesser roosters, the wing-fanning chicks and the brooding hens that it reminded one of the ways a criminal could lose himself in the melee of the *Dussehra* Procession in Mysore, making everyone a suspect.

What followed was a piece of crazy counterplot. Eight pairs of eyes went over the black, the grey, the brown, the white and the orange streaked fowls to track the jewel thief. One of them having cocked his neck, one too many times, in the manner of a nouveau riche flaunting her necklace for everyone to notice was zeroed in. They tried to corner him and he dodged their every attempt. However, he soon got isolated from the rest and had to endure a chase by eight pairs of penetrating eyes and outstretched hands, all set to grab him by his neck or whatever it took. Eventually, he was outdone by the agile detectives. They decided to keep him trapped and watch his ca-ca to retrieve the only drop of jewellery the lady possessed. But the suspect being every bit a popinjay wasn't going to poop in public, not even at the risk of inviting constipation. And the ruthless monsters were running out of patience and decided to dissect him inside out.

Do I have a choice at their hands and all for a bit of that yellow stuff? *Pixe*, he crowed through his anguish.

Then they did what they had to, said Teru. They laid open his gizzard and entrails and groped for the gem, like a set of blind men trying to define an elephant by touch. Nothing came of it and there was no way they could go after his kindred as too much time had been lost and it was next to impossible to undo their movements. For the next couple of days their mission was to look out for a shiny drop of shit.

Good Lord! An impossible lot going after a needle in a haystack, mumbled Tabby.

Chapter 3

THE AFTER ACT

I

December Blooms

Perceiving that she didn't have forever time, Teru invited the lot of them, Tabby, Blotch and Chingaari to accompany her on her saunter, before she set out on her soul journey, through the plantation for one last time. The feathered one, not quite connecting with the whims of the ex-animate declined the offer. For old times' sake, Blotch acquiesced, and Tabby was accommodating as always. An enigmatic Teru made several stop-overs to share the gleanings from the pages of her life with her friends.

At the first station, she inched up a tall mango tree, while the rest looked at her baffled for they had never seen her climbing a tree when she was alive, to uproot the wild orchids with lavender-laced white blooms named after Sita. She also eyed the more delicate ivory-coloured ones named after the legendary Rama. She put them up on an orange tree in front of her house, against their nature, quite in the manner of her children who wanted the wilds within their reach. She was pleased with her handiwork. Her companions thought, the act was absurd, but held their peace.

At the second, Teru did a roundabout like the 'Ring a Ringo' Roses...,' of the little tots which her companions couldn't resist joining in. But soon, they discovered she wasn't performing, but going in circles to avoid stepping on and occasionally skipping over those little islands of tiny butter mushrooms. She picked up a few, and turned them over in the palm of her hands, deliberating on the next course of action. Wistfully, she soon let go of them and watched them fall to the ground like a rain of jasmines. The switch of emotions from wonderment to consternation on her countenance left her companions in disarray.

Teru later filled in to say that those were the days when during a respite from the pouring rains, her children picked mushrooms from the wild, full of amazement. Teru had seasoned the delicacy with rose onions and freshly plucked green chillies. It never failed to astound the disgruntled children of how the huge pile of mushrooms was reduced to almost nothing in that sizzling pot. Teru was under compulsion to reassure them with a story of a certain mother-in-law, who having picked a pan full of mushrooms, handed them over to her daughter-in-law for seasoning. Invariably, the mother-in-law faulted her for placing titbits on the table, accusing her of having cheated her of her rightful share, ending in a fierce argument. All ears, the children savoured their portion, holding on to the creamy softness caressing their palate for the longest time possible.

At station three, walking through the dense undergrowth skirting the coffee shrubs, the birds were seen flitting from branch to branch in gay abandon. Teru gloated over the fact that her children being the fine marksmen that they were, that not even the thumb-sized humming bird escaped their pebble-shots. Picking up the game, some of them would pluck the feathers, the boys would throw open the belly with a pocketknife and empty the bowel and string the bird on a contrived skewer for roasting, she continued. The little ones would collect twigs for a fire and wait excitedly for the bird to be carved and laid out on a tender leaf wiped clean on the seat of someone's short pants. The one with deft fingers was seen drawing lots to allot portions, sometimes very tiny, at others close to a bite. For a while, all would be quiet as they ate the succulent meat and took in the organic goodness. Gratified, they patted each other on their backs, for they now belonged to the elite club of game-hunters, that their blue-blooded forefathers were. Blotch broke into a cold sweat listening to their love of *shikar* and was relieved that Chingaari, their feathered friend, had opted out of the excursion.

They are the chip off the old block, intoned Teru at station four with a replay of a dissection as in a laboratory. Whenever their father had shot a wild boar or a big game he would get it home and wake up the household to witness the ritual, she continued.

The children, got busy, piling hay over the animal and building a huge fire to burn his hair and denude him of ticks and germs, so, their father claimed, Teru recalled. And when the hay turned to ash, and the creature looked charred, their father doused the flame with water from a hosepipe.

He is ugly, grimaced the children at the sight of him.

Have you known a handsome pig ever? teased their father.

They lent a hand to roll him over onto the green banana leaves and scrubbed him clean and white. Pouting her lips Teru said,

With his lips like this, their father exfoliated him with a scrub and a shave that he now looked bald as a tonsured Brahmin widow, no longer the dirty pig he was.

Tabby and Blotch were amused at the word picture. Last came the colourful turmeric shampoo which turned him bright yellow and the children cried out,

Doesn't he look like Selvy from Madras, forever jaundiced?

The children were amazed at what their father did next. They patted his back and said,

You can easily be the envy of a surgeon, Papa.

The yucky yet precise job he did of plugging the boar's rectal orifice with a stout stub to avoid an accident; the way he clinically cut off the extremities-the ears, limbs, the tail and trotters; that straight and neat incision on the abdomen through which popped the insides and the children watching in awe was laudable, acceded Teru. He carefully brought out the entrails in one piece and showed the children the liver, the kidneys and the heart. They were astounded by the length of the intestine which was long like the road from Mysore to Mylapore. Operation accomplished, he cut out a gorgeous portion of his rump to be *tawa* fried spicing it up with loads and loads of freshly ground black pepper, lemon and salt. The ravenous dipped into the same *tawa* and relished it till done, leaving their parents to deal with the rest: cut the meat for pickling and salting; make strips to be smoke-dried; portions to be set aside for the black curry with over-roasted condiments and finally set aside allotments for distribution among the fortunate friends and neighbours. Blotch seemed agitated and wished to get home. He didn't want to be caught in the crossfire of a careless gunman of whom there were plenty in the village and be subject to the fate the boar was in. Tabby put up a brave front in emulation of his mistress and moved on.

The most laborious of all chores was to mix the coarsely lopped meat with crushed spices, vinegar and Goan *fenny* to be stuffed into the boar's cleaned, smoked and sun-dried gut skin, knotted at intervals to make sausages. The string was hung in serpentine rows over the fireplace. The children and their father were the happiest to take in the aroma of the *chorizo* that wafted through the house for as long as the stock lasted. At a loss to comprehend, Tabby asked Teru why the presence of the Oink at *Aiyya's* house kept her Mappila friends from visiting her or partaking of any meals at her house.

Not having realized that life was so fragile and dear like the December blooms, Teru had lived it as well as she could. Yet, she lingered on at the following base looking for answers to problems she hadn't fathomed in her lifetime of six years too short of ninety.

Why did my partner and I, in good times and in bad, fall apart in our old age? she asked continuing to feel rejected.

Why …, why …, why …? she lamented over issue after issue.

If resolved, of what use are the answers, as you cannot relive life anyway, ruminated Tabby.

Isn't it enough to see and know that you lived and the others lived as well, each unto his own? he wished to ask.

But given the sombre mood of his friend, and nudged by Blotch, he chose to remain mum, believing that silence would provide her with a perspective.

In a while, Teru came around and they moved on. At this scene, the sight of hundreds of those migratory green pigeons descending on the fields to eat the germinating shoots of paddy in their nursery bed, instantly engaged her mind. She asked her companions to brazen themselves against gun shots that could come from any quarter anytime to scare the birds, but what followed filled them with an unholy dread. The shot, when it was heard shattered the peace of the valley with several echo-rounds and scattered the fear-ridden birds in a thousand directions. In the confusion, Blotch who kept count of the stations they had traversed, lost the sequence and decided to hear her out all the way. And Blotch thought that he saw some of the plumed friends floating on water, having succumbed to the pellets. In the days gone by, Impey *Maama*, the friendly gunman from the neighbourhood, put the birds into a khaki rucksack. There were times when Teru's children trailed him to return home with the largesse.

Along the way, at the next post, Teru was stumped as if she were struck by a blow. Pointing to a non-existent *machan* at the far end of the terraced fields she asked Tabby if he could see it burning. Seeing neither the smoke nor the flames licking the skies, he looked at her askance. She stared for long at something her companions couldn't see. At a loss, she mumbled in a frail voice,

It's been reduced to cinders. It stood there for years, like a watchdog. The village men took turns to spend the night therein to scare away the wild boars from pillaging the ripe harvest by intermittently striking on a tin can. And now, I see that she set it on fire over a wager! For half an anna, the house is gone in a puff. What a shame!

Tabby and Blotch waited for Teru to name the culprit, which she didn't. It was so unlike her.

Teru drifted along only to stop at an overflowing open well and she ached for Andrew, a little boy of three, who had accompanied his mother to the well on her trips to fetch water, pot after pot, day after day. On that ill-fated day, the boy picked up a tiny copper pot and set out on the familiar track. Leaning over to fill the pot which refused to be immersed, he is sure to have heard it mumble something he didn't quite comprehend. He tried harder to push the pot down, resulting in his tipping into the well. The mother found him floating wide-eyed a couple of hours later, still holding on to the pot, now full. The twosome was sorry for the mother and made the sign of the cross to avert fallouts as Teru often did when in distress.

They left the base with a heavy heart and moved on to the other side of the wide expanse of lush green fields, abutting against the hilly slopes of coffee plantation, to gaze at a waterfall gushing down a rocky cliff. Here, Teru saw her children stripping themselves naked, to dive into the cavern below, and wager as to who could remain the longest under water. As they took turns to dive, the rest bathed, some washed clothes imitating their elders. The difference being, the clothes were soaked heavy with water. So much so, each time they raised them to whip on the rocky surface as a *dhobi* did, they left behind a steady circular spray of water, resembling several Ferris Wheels in motion. The others scrubbed their heels rose pink.

The oldest of them all, stood on her toes at the edge of the rocky precipice where the fall dipped, with outstretched hands over her head without as much as a stitch on herself. She stood with the readiness of a deft swimmer, waiting for the gunshot, to dive from the board. And then, she caught sight of a white vest ballooning like a parachute in the water below. It surfaced several times and then went under soon after. She saw a little hand steadfastly holding on to the balloon. She turned to look and their little brother of two frolicking on a play mat was missing. In sheer despair, she dived and got him out of the depths with his hand still clutching onto that piece of hope. The motley crew of naked bodies held him upside down and compressed his tiny lungs to squirt the water out in jerky spurts. They were relieved to see his face slowly turn from a choking ash to a living pink. A tragedy averted, sighed Teru and with a rising intonation asked,

How is that not one of them said a word about it in all these years?

It now occurred to Teru that the living had troves of secrets waiting to be unearthed in good time.

Teru was no exception to this rule. She had not breathed a word about the number of times she had lost the will to live either. A young bride with romance in her eyes and a huge baby-bump, she had been kicked around like a football. Her husband chose to show her, her place in the scheme of things in his household where his sister wanted a finger in every pie. Teru withstood the thrashing without resisting. She told herself,

The baby, the baby must not drop.

Years later, Teru died yet again, when the baby within her choked to death, burdened by a mother's ordeal. The stillborn bore six fingers and toes on each limb. Pushed to a state of comatose, Teru had battled on between life and death for weeks on end in the aftermath of the shock.

Likewise, the last straw came and when it did, Teru saw herself running out of course. The revelation that her husband of forty-eight years had made no provision for her in his will broke her spirit. Then on, life to her was a mere whiff of air and she wished to give up the ghost and death continued to dodge her. But now that she was dead, she was fighting to flee from it. Clinical death wasn't the end of the road either. There was this reckoning to contend with. Aggrieved as she was in life, there was no recourse to redressal in death, she complained. Life had been full of upheavals. As in life, death too posed challenges. She couldn't see an escape hatch. Teru's life wasn't hers at all at any stage, to live it as it pleased her. The prospect devastated her.

Blotch was not clear on the stand he was expected to take. It was against his nature to champion the cause of men against men. His species suffered from no such concerns and contemplating on the past was alien to him. He didn't believe in, '*heaven's high city*,' either, but *carpe diem*. Leaving Teru to her own reflections, he got busy darting after the seasonal fruit flies dancing over an overripe, rain soaked jackfruit on the ground. When he could eat no more, he looked up to find Teru and Tabby inch along towards the other side of the cliff. Open mouthed, he leapfrogged to catch up with them. In the process, a few flies escaped from his puffed-up belly.

Once within earshot of them, he heard Teru tell Tabby of the jackfruit *patioie* she had wrapped in banana leaves and steamed. The preparation was so akin to the making of the sweet *tamales* in Mexico, the visiting missionary had stated. The children loved them for their fruity taste and the crunchy coconut chips they bit into with every mouthful. The children received six pieces each and had the freedom to gobble them at once or ration them out.

How the children ran around the house to hide their share from the rest, Teru mused.

The one who had managed to stretch his stock the most was envied and watched closely as he savoured his bites. Often, he got an edge over the others by switching his hideouts and replenishing his stock with appropriated allotments. The fights that broke out to square accounts seemed irreconcilable. Abashed, the defeated kicked the family dog *Beedi* and cursed him,

You scoundrel, watch out, you will soon grow a pot belly so large that it will rip open to show up the filcher that you are; with your stuffed stomach, you are sure to bring on yourself nightmares so terrible that you will have no place to hide in; and may you rot in hell for depriving us of our lot.

And all the while, the curser avoided eye contact with the suspected *patioie chor*. A direct confrontation, he feared, would have a backlash. The lambasting amused Teru, but not the duo in her company. They said,

Confound the lot of them, they mean not what they say, and they say it to them whom they mean it not for.

Through the *tamasha*, Beedi did not flinch in the least. It didn't mean that Beedi had grown apathetic to their abuses. Occasionally, he would appear confused and be forced to lower his head, roll his eyeballs and snivel almost tearfully.

II

Living in Shackles

You did ask me, what sort of name that is, 'Beedi '? stated Teru.

Well, he is a pariah. Named so, as occasionally he shared a puff of the beedi with his mistress Subbi, of the Kuruba tribe. When the Kurubas made off at night with their chattels and their hunting gear in search of fresh grounds for foraging roots, berries and game and to dodge shame, Beedi got left behind. He whined for his mistress for the next eight days. It was so heart rending that Teru's heir brought him home on his shoulder, like a shepherd would the young lost lamb. He was ever so grateful that he ate and slept with his new master and followed his every step. Once, his master having been hospitalized for chronic stomach runs, Beedi was overcome with a foreboding so terrible that he filled the house with his dolorous whining. He sat on his master's bed and would let none of the household to attend to him, not until his master's return.

That's Beedi for you, said she.

Approaching the ensuing station, it was Teru's turn to cross herself.

Holy Mother of God! she cried out.

Teru heard a pack of mongrels yelping at first and then baying only to retreat with consternation.

Is it my otherworldliness that makes these dogs go hammer and tongs or are they baffled by Tabby's presence? And a flinching Blotch can't wait to make good his escape, thought a distressed Teru looking for a safe exit from the volatile scene.

Bite-sized that I'm, I'll be finished in one gulp. Let's scoot, he said and in utter confusion turned a three-sixty degree and hopped with supersonic speed.

Harried, Tabby hurried along, with not a word said. A duel between the canines and the felines invariably ended with someone losing an eye or with a broken neck. Teru didn't wish to linger around either. At this stop, she would have liked to show her associates what buck teethed Kunhchiamina looked like. Her every incisor was almost an inch in length and to make room for itself had pushed the other out of alignment. She was gigantic with long flapping breasts that tapped her bulbous abdomen with every step she took. She had set her mind on Abdullah who was half her size. She displaced the mother of his two children with the Indian *ghol* chilli paste. Teru didn't wish to elaborate on the many uses the paste could be put to. She sensed death lurking around Kunhchiamina's house in the guise of a terminal illness, giving the shrew a taste of the invincible potency of karmic settlement of scores.

Teru rambled on, only to come to a standstill at an empty post, to stare at the Kuruba hutments that once were. Subbi's kith had lived there for over three generations, but on their own terms. Their local landlady, a widow, had no sway over their lives. They worked for the widow at will and when they were fancy free. Born to the wild, they were content. A day or two of work gave them ready cash to fetch salt and clothes. They were their own doctors and teachers and lived by the tenets and wisdom handed down by their forefathers. They were apathetic to the folks on the other side of the fence. In public, their gaze was lowered and their tongue muted, always.

A Kuruba's back was covered with minimal clothes: a plain shirt, a pair of threadbare short pants with bulging pockets and a seamless length of cloth over his shoulder. One cloth, many uses. It served as a net to trap and lug wild fish from streams, as a sieve to squeeze out the honey from the combs gathered in the woods, a makeshift bag to transport soap nuts, mangoes, taro roots and jackfruit pods to his hut. And of course, his embellishments: a catapult around his neck, a bow and a quiver full of arrows on his back and the amulet on his arms, each crafted with the utmost care by every Kuruba.

In contrast, the women folk were bare shouldered. They draped the sari so unlike others. It barely covered their knees and the top end was pulled over diagonally across the bosom with the left shoulder serving as an anchor to hold it in place. A string of bright beads entangled with a knotty string, twisted several times over by some holy man to ward off evil, adorned their necks.

A picture of the Kuruba's once-a-day trip to the little town for a cup of that frothy sugary *chai* at **Umar Kaka's** hotel could easily find a pride of place in the Louvre. The elder, a man bent double by the ravages of time, led the clan with the rest following him in hierarchical order, with the youngest at the trail end. A joey would either get a ride on a man's shoulder or go piggy on his mother's back, held in place by a length of cloth looped around her shoulder and waist. They would walk across the plain barefoot, clamber down the inclines of the plantation, trek along the meandering dykes among the fields of paddy pregnant with ripe grain and surge up another of those hills to come down to a serpentine tarred road. Like the saffron clad Buddhist monks walking along the sides of the Kandy Lake, in a linear formation on their way to the temple of the Sacred Tooth Relic, these Kurubas walked to the town in equal earnest, keeping to one side of the road. On arrival, they huddled around the table to be served their portion of *chai* depending on the money the elder spilt on the table with a jingle from his greasy pouch. With diligence, they would slurp the tea by turns from their share of one or two of those ribbed glasses, their due. It was done with such single-minded intent that the tea could almost be seen being drawn from the cup to the lip in an unbroken stream. The tribe conscious Kuruba barely mouthed the cup.

Among them was a pair of siblings whom the onlookers didn't miss. Siddu, a boy with a mop of curls which bounced with his every step and Seethe just about breaking into womanhood. The widow's moustache twirling son, having returned home after his tenure in the army, was stirred by this child woman. Nicknamed Military *Mishey,* he got the duo to serve him at his mother's palatial bungalow. At his bidding, they washed his clothes, polished his shoes and those prized brass buckles, dusted his furniture, and assisted him in cleaning the barrels of his rifle, tugging the bore brush attached to a string. The pair, out of fear didn't cast as much as a glance at him. Schemingly, he set out individual targets for completion and Siddu had harder and time-consuming chores to attend to.

Military *Mishey* the predator and privileged one, chose Seethe for his carnal gratification and appropriated her body and desecrated her soul. She was paralyzed by the violation. A little before sunset, Seethe trudged home, crushed and muted by the tear, the bleeding and the humiliation. At dusk, her grandmother was at the same waterfall frequented by Teru's children, applying turmeric paste on Seethe's naked and ravaged body while the other women were standing in a circle around them. They beat their breasts and wailed moan-fully, and sprinkled water on her from little branches of neem to wash away her defilement. The world around stood still and watched, indifferent, unmoved, by the pathos of a people who had no recourse to redressal.

At day break, the widow discovered that the Kurubas had razed their hutments to the ground and had deserted the place. No answers to the questions, 'Why?' or 'Where to?' As ordained, Beedi who had gone on a jaunt with the strays in the neighbourhood at the time of their nocturnal flight, got left behind.

Nine months later, Seethe became a child mother of a girl who belonged every inch to the warrior clan like her father. The infant had a nose marked by a bow-shaped septum, a broad forehead, high cheekbones and a buttery complexion not known to her tribe. A Kuruba usually turned the other way when a curious outsider stopped to stare at the moppet born on the wrong side of the blanket.

She lives to tell a muffled tale, thought the knowing.

Soon after, her mother was found hanging from an orange tree, with no reasons sought by either man or God.

It doesn't come as a surprise, said a despondent Teru.

Seethe's favourite goddess by choice, the Thamme of Pannangala, was herself a scapegoat of a deeply entrenched patriarchal mind-set. The vulnerable Thamme is as helpless when it came to championing Seethe's cause, sighed Teru.

Legends vouchsafe for Thamme a place among the pantheon of goddesses. Yet, she was disowned by Igguthappa who deigned her unfit for the status of a revered deity, for nearly having outperformed her brothers, even if in jest. No tears could abrogate Thamme's woes and it thus became her fate to receive obeisance from the casteless *Holeyas* whose ghettos were immersed in the stench of their body odour and hooch.

Teru leaning on a boulder, with Tabby crowning it and Blotch at her feet listening, she recreated a scene that pushed a sister to the brink of despair.

The seven brothers and a sister, born not of flesh, crossed the seven seas, she began, four of whom put down roots in Kodagu. Having walked the distant mile from Kerala to reach Ambla Pole, they were famished.

Igguthappa then said,

Sister dear, will you cook a meal for me? I'm hungry.

I shall, but there is no rice to cook a meal and no fuel for a fire, she replied.

I shall provide the rice. Will you cook it without the fire? he challenged her.

Naan thithillathe kuul beppi, ninga uppillathe uumbira? she retorted.

Tabby and Blotch were quite up to the dare and waited for the outcome. Blotch, however, had a hunch that in matters to do with the kitchen, the women always had an advantage. Thamme validated her prowess by accepting Igguthappa's challenge. She soaked the rice in rolling hot milk and left it on scorching sand and her job was done. But the brothers found it unpalatable to gulp down the bland rice without salt. They waxed poetic and hurled the rice skyward saying,

Here's a hail shower,
Rice without salt
Is,
Like a garden without blooms,
A nest without birds,
And a face without a smile.

So much for her trouble, thought Tabby.

The aggrieved Thamme didn't take to it kindly. She got hold of a ladle and whacked the brothers on their backs and cried out,

And here's the thunderclap to announce the hail shower.

Pleased with having outwitted her brothers, she sat down to ceremoniously roll the *paan* with a heady mixture of areca, *chunam,* candy sugar and flavoured shavings of *copra.* For the next couple of minutes, all was still as the siblings rolled the mingle-mangle in their mouths to release the beet-red juice. Every attempt was made to hold it in, to prevent the red stream of spittle rolling down their chins in little rivulets. Each ounce of it counted in the run up to the red-jet spitting contest where they tried to outdo the other.

As a prerequisite to the contest, they began to provoke each other with a show of their ruddy tongues and lips. At one point, the contest got so tough that they held up the spittle in their left palms for collation of scores. The ruddier, the better they boasted choking on the reserve in their mouths. Having qualified to the final jet-spitting round, all the contestants passed their hands back over their left shoulders to chuck the vermillion stuff. Their young sister did likewise, except that she returned the caste demeaning fluid into her mouth, with incredulous outcome.

The brothers instantly denounced her fallen.

Not even an imbecile would return the spittle into her mouth. Your degradation is therefore of your own making. There is no redemption for you. Leave us you must and pay for your abomination by becoming the goddess of the marginalized, Igguthappa thundered.

Here the *Holeya* untouchable, the brothers declaimed.

The wretched Thamme's grief knew no bounds. She wept, she pleaded, but her position remained irredeemable as her brothers didn't relent.

To this day, she continues to be worshipped by devotees forced upon an unwilling goddess, ended Teru. Not so unlike Seethe who continues to be rejected for bringing shame to her tribe, as inadvertently.

And you deem that Seethe is caught between the devil and the deep sea, repeated a confused Blotch.

It simply means that Seethe had no recourse to a benevolent goddess for solace. Besides, she was vulnerable at the hands of men of caste with no prudence, explained Tabby.

Teru tried to nod her stiff head at the discourse. In a while, Teru resumed her narration. Annually, the Kurubas who are placed above the rest on the caste grid, go on a pilgrimage to Devarakadu at Hebbale, not so much to pray, but as much to abuse the goddess of their tribe Bhagavathi for eloping with Aiyappa and forsaking them, at the hands of their slave driver masters.

Seethe couldn't count on Bhagavathi in her fall from grace either, could she? And there, now the same goddess, deserving of a string of those abuses, is foisted upon the Kurubas to be worshipped, posited Teru.

A double whammy indeed, she further affirmed.

But why would anyone want to abuse their gods? asked a bewildered Blotch.

On what they call the 'Feast of the Rumps,' continued Teru ignoring his question, the men in Seethe's tribe drown themselves in hooch to loosen their tongues and give vent to their ill will. On such days, I've seen their women and children running helter-skelter from being groped and pinched on the rumps and elsewhere in an unseemly manner. I've seen them spending the day hiding in the trenches among the coffee bushes. Outsiders are not spared either.

On such occasions, Teru's husband, hurried back from his early round of the check-rolls on the estate, to warn his household of the fiends on the move. On their way to the temple, they danced around the houses in the village to the sound of eerie tunes coming out of those pear-shaped bottle gourds, handcrafted drums and bamboo shells. The women would hurry through their chores and make sure the doors were secured in time. Quite like the town on the Grecian Urn, the entire village took on a deserted look through the day.

He was not the familiar Kuruba I had known, announced Teru.

You should see to believe the metamorphosis of the otherwise docile community. Reeking of hooch, they looked you squarely in the eye. When they dared to bare their teeth, I saw that they were the same colour as their eyes, ruddy, she decried.

Moving in circles, they chanted in the most vilifying terms,

Kunde, kunde,
Look at her pearly teeth,
Kunde kunde,
Look at her swaying hips.

Refrain:
Kunde kunde, kunde kunde

Look at her breasts, so round,
Like cream, whipped,
Don't miss her lobes, bejeweled,
I like it nibbled.

Kunde kunde, kunde, Kunde

Look at her *doresaani* face, so white,
Look at her hair so like floss,
Look at her rump, such a delight,
Look at her plump gherkin toes.

Kunde kunde, kunde kunde

    If you happened to be an aspiring graduate attending a University or if you were a career woman they chorused,

College *kunde,*
Office *kunde,*
Madame *kunde,*
Hullkot kunde.

Kunde kunde, kunde kunde.

All the while they snapped their fingers at their victims and went about like a bull on a rampage.

Livid as the Kuruba might have been at the injustice heaped on him, Teru's household listened with bated breath and never did they let a whimper escape their lips. Her children, intrigued as they were with the sprightly choral dancing, and not wanting to waste any of that hair-raising music, formed an inner circle of their own within the four walls of the house and in muted breath shimmied to the refrain of, *Kunde Kunde*, narrated Teru.

When the hapless Kurubas had said and done enough to avenge their *kismet*, they moved on to Hebbale to berate Bhagavathi and Aiyappa, to give them a tongue lashing for having let them down and the vulnerable Seethe. There, it was more of the same. More *hooch*, spiked *paan*, more of the clamorous music, more dance and relentless abuse. Gradually petering out, they walked in a trance on imaginary embers to help in the purification of their tainted tribe. Rankled with evil thoughts and ill will towards god and man, they now sought forgiveness for the irreverence they had heaped on their gods and prayed for the repose of Seethe's soul.

On their return home, a Kuruba kept a low profile as usual till it was time to go around once again, blaspheming all and sundry, *Kunde Kunde*.

Drawn to the unusual sound of, *Croande, Croande, Croande*, Teru looked around to realize that Blotch was in his elements at her feet and was hopping in circles, holding up his wrinkled bottom in an upward tilt. When Teru reprimanded him for his public display of vulgarity, he began to hop away, a few leaps at a time and was heard muttering,

I'm half Kuruba, for I've eaten the leftovers from their tapping of honey. I love their poetics, even Plato would have lauded them for their plain-speak.

Taken by surprise, Tabby grimaced at his earthiness.

After all you live in a hole, he chided and skipped down the boulder and walked abreast of Teru.

Blotch was intrigued and didn't quite understand Teru's account of why Seethe's rudderless soul was known to haunt the place. It was rumoured that she sought retribution to smite Military *Mishey* for having despoiled her. Speculations were rife that on the day she got him alone, she would pluck his heart out and feed it to the reluctant vultures. Blotch had only two shades to his reading on the issue: Seethe was either alive or dead. Whereas to Tabby, though Teru was morgue cold, she was not altogether dead, not yet, not for as long as he could relate to her.

Seethe had been schooled by her grandmother who had regaled her with tales of a time when the Kuruba had the reign over the forest. In better times, a Kuruba came looking for his bride on horseback and whisked her away from right under the nose of his future father-in-law, seldom having to put up a fight. Such daring and courage were admirable qualities which made him eligible for the hand of his maiden daughter. A Kuruba, not being able to measure up to the characteristic chivalry and the cultural clout of the times gone by, in due course all a bride came to expect was a coarsely spun sari and an elopement in tow. The couple would spend the ensuing days in hiding among the coffee bushes. When their energies were spent, they would emerge as a married couple and life would go on, bound by no compulsions for ceremonies and feasts.

The excursion having come a full circle, the trio contemplated on what Seethe's final thoughts may have been as life was snuffed out of her?

III

The Umbilical Tug

Bitten to the bone by a chill known only to the dead, Teru lamented,

The sand is running out and I have a myriad concerns to resolve, before I sleep among the dead.

Foremost, Teru wished to rip past her mother's home town in Chickpet, a place where her ancestors had put down roots, having been taken prisoners by the Sultan two centuries ago, after his fall at the hands of the English in Seringapatam. She was grateful to

Dodda Veerarajendra, the then ruler of Kodagu, for the hospitality bestowed on her ancestors.

How she loved her mother's quaint home with the thatched roof, almost like Hannah Hathaway's. It had a veranda that ran all around the house resembling a ring road. The lightly carved pillars at intervals, supporting the stooping roof, served as posts for children to play the game of Crisscrossing to the Post. It was played by changing posts, cutting across along the length and breadth of the veranda, scoring a home run by avoiding elimination. The more the number of players, the merrier the game became.

Teru remembered the times when she fought her way through to find room on the Raja Seat, built into a corner of the veranda, against the wall. It could house no more than three little pairs of buttocks at a time. When a fourth sought a place, he or she had to play push bottoms and invariably the one seated at the open end of the seat was nudged out. The seat was made of patted dirt and polished with a slurry of cow dung, yet it looked so regal that were a Maharaja to pass that way, he would no doubt have coveted it for his own.

Seated there, Teru had often seen a man from town come by, day after day, before twilight, to replenish oil in the lamps suspended on the lamp-posts and light them for the night. And scores of insects hovered around the flame, only to shed their wings and drop down to die, all in a matter of hours.

On days when Teru was early to rise, she had seen gorgeous looking English women clad in slacks and turtle-neck pullovers ride past on their equally groomed horses.

Teru had witnessed wedding processions pass by with demure Christian brides in their *sado* and at times a Kodava groom in his royal *kuppasa*. The accompanying *kombu kottu* and *volaga* gave her the goose bumps and made her look for a groom in the crowd, whom she wished to marry at once. But she didn't like to relive the story of a man who had asked for an extra serving of the black pork curry at a wedding reception. His request having been turned down, the inebriated guest drew his ornamental *kaththi* from the silver holster on his waist band and stabbed the waiter to death.

At Teru's father's house, the only thing the children had to keep away from, was his four-post bed which was centred below a rocking basket hanging from the roof. Years later, she discovered the reason for it. Here it was, where her father hid his savings along with the nasty smelling cashew liquor during the lean days of prohibition. He claimed, it helped him suppress his bouts of cough.

In the centre of that compact home was what then seemed like a humongous receptacle, a mud wattle, rising from the floor and almost reaching the ceiling. It was made of splintered cane interlocked and plastered with dung to store paddy and other provision for the year. Often Teru would climb the ladder to get to the loft and jump into the well- like chamber to explore the possibilities it held.

Teru ached for the times when the three sisters huddled together in the forbidden receptacle to eavesdrop on their parents having a showdown. Teru relished the way they traded charges of shame and debauchery, blow for blow. *Mai* said,

You come from a stock of inebriated men. It's a disgrace that your father and his six siblings drank themselves to the grave and you are the chip off that old block. You have handed over your land to the neighbouring Kodava in exchange for *soro* with not a penny to show for it.

Her husband pulled himself tall through his short breaths and said,

You fishmonger, not a word more from you, you who is a *Sudra*. Had I known that, I'd never have considered your offer of marriage.

But in good times, they were the best of friends. The man told his wife, of his household where the seven brothers lived with their seven wives in a house with a central courtyard and a tiled roof resembling the *imane* of the Kodavas. They were the thousand *batti* Britto's from Kavaadi. The women of that household took turns to cook. When the menfolk sat down cross-legged on the mats to dine, they invariably found strands of hair or grit in the rice and the curry turned out to be either too salty or pungent to stomach. Well, the lady in charge of the cooking for the day was hauled up by her husband to later emerge from her room with a black eye and a bloody face. The other women kept a straight face and there was no telling who was behind the malicious act of tarnishing the image of the one getting too big for her boots.

One rotten apple is enough to contaminate the lot of them, reckoned Teru.

Soon the entire household fell apart and their standing became part of history and they are heard of no more. Teru's maternal grandmother, on the other hand, came to Kedumullur as a young bride, riding on a bullock cart for days on end, all the way from the snobbish coast of Kodial. Family legends speak of her having come not only with a rich trousseau but also a little ceramic jar full of gold and several *murrahas* of rice, rock salt, sun dried balls of tamarind, oil and jaggery, fearing that she could die of starvation in a land where life was hard and cold, besides being infested with mosquitoes. The stock was meant to last her till she found her bearings to fend for herself and her new household. She was the talk of the town for a while till others followed in her wake, married to men whom they had never known and worse seen, except from the corner of their eyes on their way up the aisle. The matches were made by a mutual elder on whom depended the happiness of the guileless couple. And folklore genealogists vouched for it that she was every bit a *Bamonn* as her husband was and the matter of caste and class were soon laid to rest.

A contemplative Teru was drawn to the stone trough standing in the same place as of yore, adjacent to the entryway of the house, below the awning. For years, it held fresh water for folks from the village, to wash their muddy feet before entering town, Teru's house being placed at the intersection between the two.

Recollection of Sundays at her mother's house made her wistful. She was fussed over by *Mai* who gave her a ritual bath and prepared her for the Sunday service. Her hair was freshly oiled and parted to be plaited into two thick braids and bound with colourful ribbons which bounced on her buttocks as she walked to church. *Mai* then got busy steaming heaps and heaps of fluffy rice *sannas* in plates mounted over each other, with bamboo sticks placed in between to make room and keep them from smudging their snow-white faces. Some of them would be topped with grated jaggery and finely scraped coconut. When done, they were spread out on the dining table on an intricately woven bamboo tray covered with muslin.

Why so many *Mai*, is there going to be a wedding in the house? the children asked.

You will see, was all she said.

And then came the parishioners from the far off Kedumullur, having walked across fields, circumventing the bottomless *Pathalakolli* and wading through a stream. They washed themselves at the stone trough and came in smelling of her mother's green soap put out only for her Sunday guests. They would then busy themselves applying Remy snow on their faces and topping them with Ponds talcum powder. Dressed in their Sunday best, they marched off another mile or two to St. Ann's on paved roads. Two hours later, on their way back, they made one more stop at *Mai's* to undress and get into their plain clothes before helping themselves to rice bread and a glass of that clear black coffee for a dip. The memory of the aromatic flat cakes of jaggery used to sweeten the coffee and flavour it, tingled Teru's taste buds. In her present state, Teru nearly slurped with a sense of vicarious pleasure. Coffee Day that her grandchildren so raved about could not get anywhere close to that authentic taste, she thought.

Teru was disappointed to see that her childhood house no longer stood, but in its place, was a garish concrete structure. A way of life had been replaced by Porsches and Pulsars. And there were no more visits and gifts from the people of the village. In the days gone by, the humble folk came with a rooster and some home-grown eggs, a stubby broom with a butt full of fingertip-sized rosettes in white, on the tip end of the silky fine grass stalks of which it was rolled, all for *Mai*. Occasionally, the children were gifted a kitten, a pair of chicks or a pup.

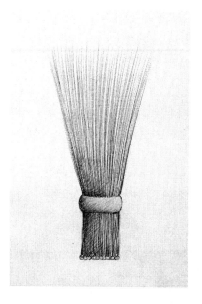

Teru peered into the narrow backyard which now appeared shrunk for some reason. The sole coconut tree that had stood the test of time had been razed to the ground, struck by lightning, she had learnt. The rose apple and the blue berry trees stood, and in place of the leech pit, stood an English latrine. With that, the acidic stench from the pit, which came and went with the fanning wind was gone too.

Teru regretted the way *Mai* had pulled out her brood from school for no fault of theirs. An older sibling, the one with eyes which were round, bright and watchful too, like those of a meerkat sensing a predator, had stopped by on her way to school to watch Rama, a monkey, performing tricks. Puckering her forehead in imitation of Rama, she got too close to him for comfort and goggled into his eyes. Peeved as he was at having to dance to his masters tune at the break of day, he bit off a generous portion of her pink cheek. Of course, she came to be known as 'Monkey Mary' forthwith and no man worth his salt was willing to marry the cheek-less one. It was such a shame that *Mai* had them confined to the walls of her house and Teru's schooling ended even before it had begun.

On that night, a long time ago, Monkey Mary was smarting at the prospect of having to witness her sister Monica, younger to her by a year, all set to walk up the aisle. The night before the nuptials, the sisters went to bed early, on mattresses rolled out on the floor. The bride had her long tresses washed and spread out on her pillow for airing, to be braided and rolled into a coiffure, the following morning. At cocks crow, the house came to life, with a country band playing wedding songs at their door step to the accompaniment of the *volaga*, waking up the girls and the neighbourhood to an expectant day. And *Mai* came into sound the bride. An eager bride rolled to her side and sat up to find that the right side of her head felt weightless. To her distress, she found her cascading locks lying on her pillow, having been snipped off unevenly.

The crestfallen women had neither the time nor Mary's malice to guess the name the folks were going to dub her with. Monica could be a, 'half head, a nitwit, a ....?' They had a trying time to keep the loathsome act under wraps with *mogrem* and *abolim* included till the last of the wedding guest had left.

Was her untimely and partial tonsure a sign of what was to come? reflected the household on hindsight.

Five years into her marriage, she was already a mother of two and the third delivery brought in the twins which didn't augur well for any of them. Within days of each other, the twins were gone and so did Monica, their mother. Teru remembered how her sister was laid out with the infants on either side of her for public viewing.

Bidding adieu to a way of life which had been reduced to a memory, Teru decided to walk on to Ann's. For one last time, Teru longed to go up the spiral staircase to the choir loft at the rearmost end of the church, housing the grand piano and watch the bells peal the angelus from close quarters. With cheerful readiness, she walked up two steps at a time. To her astonishment, when she got there, she thought she saw the silhouette of a man with a hoary beard hitting the ivory keys. She did an about turn and made a dash out of the place, along the winding circuit, gliding down the banister.

Simultaneously, the pair of bells began to peal the angelus. Threatened by the unexpected presence of an apparition, the wave after wave of the resonating echo of the bells from the tower and the hives of bees at the belfry that raked up a buzzing ruckus, she wished she were both blind and deaf. On exit, she kept running down the slope, down the hill till she came to a convent across the road, where she paused gasping for breath. It was sometime before she noticed a gradual movement behind the stained-glass panes. She looked up and felt at home to see the sisters of Tarbes walking in a single file along the passage, with hands tucked under their aprons and their faces blinkered by stiff bonnets. They were chanting the vespers. Terror-riven as she was, the soulful rendition soothed her nerves. She decided to join Tabby at the funeral home.

Teru's only regret was that she couldn't rummage through the sacristy where the religious artefacts were stored. She would have given an arm and a leg for one look at the *kuttumbolichcha* gifted to the church by the magnanimous Dodda Veerarajendra. One last look at the lamp that had lit her church and warmed her heart was all she yearned for, to bid goodbye to a way of life.

IV

Walk Alone

I have lived through much and have died many times over. All that I'm left with is the now, Teru said to herself with resignation.

Tabby and Blotch had never seen her so woeful and wondered what had gone amiss. They stared at her in disbelief, as she no longer seemed ecstatic about life and she wasn't even fighting for an extra breath. In fact, like Blotch, she appeared blanched. Her forehead, the corners of her lips and her nail beds were like a mosaic of blue and white. Tabby made room for Teru at the fire place thinking that the warmth could infuse some life into her damp spirit. Leaving her to come out of her blues, he hopped on to the table in the centre of the drawing room, to check for moths hovering about the smelly kerosene lamp with a bulbous globe. He tried to mouth an insect with a transparent wingspan but to no avail, and in fact, he came away with singed whiskers and a burnt nose.

So much for a cat from a town, an epic failure at antics, mumbled Blotch.

And Teru was nowhere to be seen. Blotch hadn't kept an eye on her either. Not sure of what to make of it, Tabby sat crouched on the window sill. Between catnaps, he looked about with one open eye and happened to glance at the mirror on the wall, for a second time. There he saw the same old tunnel which rolled out a moving tale. He recognized the Reverend by his hoary beard, the bony man by his gangly legs, and Teru's father by his striped pyjamas, accompanied by an entourage and a host of petite lemon-yellow butterflies. He wasn't sure if Teru was part of the Spirit Pageant.

Tabby decided to keep vigil all night, if only to make sure of Teru's whereabouts. That's when he decided to eavesdrop on a telephone conversation between Teru's offspring No.8. who was drawing comfort from No.1., an older sibling.

No.8: Just two more days to go for the Weeks Mind, hope Mama's soul will soon find repose after all that she went through in life.

No.1: What do you think? She must be up there somewhere giving him as good as she got it!

No. 8: You mean it's not over yet. And all his bullying will boil down to a counter bullying before Gods? I don't envy him his master's voice.

No.1: Remember the times he used to wield his double barrel gun and threaten to take pot-shots at Mother, …

Good Lord! I don't like such threats, said Tabby and crossed his heart out of habit, something he had learnt to do having lived with Teru.

No.8: Sure, I do. I thought the threats were for real and was petrified at the prospect of having to grow up without mother.

No.1: And, I remember her threat of jumping into the well. She walked out with you in her arms in the dead of night. No one stopped her, not even him. I went after her to discover that she was walking in the direction of the cowshed for shelter instead. We spent the night among the cud chewing, dung dropping, and bladder emptying bovines who kept staring at us all night.

No.8: He didn't have it his way either, not all the time anyway? I wondered what it was that made her break free and come out up front to challenge his clout over her, in her twilight years. At times, she ticked him off holding court, which necessitated his running for cover.

No.1: Oh, yes, for someone who didn't know the difference between a lieutenant and a foot soldier, I marvel at the tall tale she came up with. She looked him up squarely in the eye and told him that a Captain was in love with her and had plans to marry her.

Tabby was amused. He was plain curious to know how on earth Teru was going to manage that with her husband still looming large in her life.

No.8: I can't imagine mother at four feet nothing, at seventy, with that potbelly of hers, walking up the aisle with a Captain in full-dress uniform. And where did this Captain surface from in the one-horse town she lived in, anyway?

No.1: What a beating his ego took. That she, a subordinate dared to challenge his hold over her, disregarding the wedding band.

No.8: You mean he believed her, come along Sis, how could he?

No.1: Oh no. He fake-believed so that he had one more whip to thrash her with, and did she care? To make matters worse, she told him that he would be invited to church to see her walk down the aisle. Her grown up children laughed into their sleeves at the theatricals that followed.

No.8: The poor man is cornered, with no support coming, from neither the gods nor the demons. So, it is universally, each unto his own here and the hereafter. Is that how the curtains are brought down after life?

No.1: And why not, even God wouldn't want to be caught on the wrong side of heavenly dispensation, not in these times under the glare of the media and the human rights advocates, would He?

So, the sisters went on with their light-hearted banter. Tabby was comforted in the knowledge that Teru would sort out her life even if it were at the end of her journey.

Chapter 4

TWIGGING HER YESTERDAYS

I

The Feline Perspective

Teru dies.

Teru had gone missing beyond trace. Tabby so inferred. Why else would he not have seen her anywhere, not even at the cemetery where the mound of dirt was still fresh over her remains? Such anxiety made him shed his coat. He stood upright and cast one last look around and gave himself a thorough shake up from his whiskers to the tip of his tail. He then berated himself,

Be true unto yourself. A feline is not allowed expectations and therefore you sleep sound.

All the same, there was Blotch and he couldn't resist drawing him into a discourse.

What do you think? he asked.

Me? I think nothing, was his brusque reply.

Tabby was troubled and wanted to make sure that Teru was on her way to wherever she needed to go and not stray.

What if she is seated under a tree to discern the next course of her journey and not find an answer? Tabby wondered aloud.

You mean like the Buddha? came an unexpected rejoinder.

Nothing said, each went his way to spend the night in his corner of the house. And each had a dream and they compared notes on waking up. Blotch had seen something the size of an egg mysteriously working itself inward like the caterpillar and disappear altogether from sight. Tabby on the other hand, was blessed by the sight of a tall gooseberry tree, with a canopy of a million glow worms. Blotch spent the night croaking regretfully at not having had a bite of whatever it was which was rolling itself inward incessantly and Tabby spent his, trying to count the shifting creatures. But the question loomed large,

Where is Teru?

Life is obscure for mankind, thought Tabby. Notwithstanding the philosophies of Sartre and Camus, man's existential dilemma seemed unresolved. Nevertheless, Tabby thought with pride that his mistress had put up a brave front and managed to live a life of dignity despite many restraints.

Tabby conceded that it was now time for Teru to introspect and discern the life she had lived and validate it. On second thoughts, he supposed that she must have gone into meditation, a luxury she was denied here on earth. And she was unlikely to find answers, unless she extricated herself from the rubble of human concerns including those in the realm of her present ambit. That meant that the bony man could now breathe a sigh of relief.

II

Reading Signs

Altogether stranded, Tabby began to reminisce about his kitten-hood days for solace. A time when he had heard of the matriarch from Grandpa's family who walked the children outdoors before the twilight hour. He was curious to meet this Grandaunt of Kenny and Glen if only to fathom the whereabouts of Teru. Tabby found her sitting on the topmost flight of steps leading to a well, weaving garlands from the delicately scented jasmine buds picked by the little hands.

As the misty hour closed in on them, Tabby saw Grandaunt pointing to the sky above and tell Kenny and Glen of a grandfather star who was watching them grow up and a mother star minding her infant child. She then showed them a cluster of clouds which assumed the shape she gave them. She pointed to what looked like a black and white magpie with a long tail and said,

Serves him right, he is pitched to that spot to constrain him to give up his habit of pilfering and hoarding.

And what of that sheep Grams? asked the lad.

Well, he was not inclined to listen to mama sheep and jumped the fence. There he goes, stuck till he is sorry, right? said Grandaunt continuing to spin more tales.

Is it like a time-out? asked Kenny.

Maybe or maybe not, added Grandaunt waiting for the message to sink in.

How's that Elizabeth Terry was a black cloud yesterday and today she has moved higher and looks ivory white seated next to Grandpa cloud? What is she so cheerful about? asked Glen, the chirpy brother of the pigtailed girl.

Well, she made trouble for bony Grandpa when she was younger. Now that she is sorry, Grandpa doesn't mind having her next to him. If they become good friends as all siblings ought to, it is possible that the two of them will move higher and higher to a dazzling white cloud and get to shake hands with the Reverend at the Pearly Gates, someday soon.

You mean Peter the Reverend? asked Kenny.

A slow smile spread over Tabby's face only to be retarded by two factors: a singed nose painfully bordered with stubbly whiskers and a heavy heart eased at the thought of being able to trace Teru.

III

Soul Speak

That could be it, reasoned Tabby.

Losing no time, Tabby hopped down the sill into the yard and took a good look at the sky, to see on which of those supple seats Teru was perched. He was lost like the time he was counting those fireflies on the gooseberry tree.

There are too many hovering souls dodging the penitential rites, Tabby thought alarmed.

He had to get through the maze to find Teru. He was hopeful that those around would lead him to her, if only he could track them.

For sure, that's Mai, who Teru was so fond of. Didn't she have a face like a wrinkled walnut? he purred with delight at his detective skill.

Would lanky Monica show up with her twins? **he revelled** with expectation.

Monkey Mary would be cheek-less for a fact, **he grimaced.**

The exemplar, Tabby didn't remember having seen him as part of that Spirit Pageant. He could still be on the terrestrial plain, hovering about in readiness to escort Teru when she opts to join those seeking atonement.

Will Aan, who took pride in his daughter Teru, be there to watch her scale the heights? Teru said that he was always dressed in striped pyjamas when at home, didn't she? **he recalled.**

And good old Aaleema, Teru's midwife, she was raw-boned. She had an infectious laughter and her teeth were stained red from chewing paan, that's a great clue, **he gloated.**

Didn't Grandaunt also tell Kenny and Glen that those who had gone before grandpa and for that matter even Aan and Mai would also turn up to receive their flock, post atonement? Tabby contemplated.

But, there is always a catch, *Mai* had cautioned in a conspiratorial tone.

Once among the rung of clouds, there is no surveillance. The souls are on their own. Souls are expected to discriminate the afflictions mankind endure with great probity. It could take the souls time and effort to speak the truth and shame the devil.

Tabby noticed that bony Grandpa who appeared grouchy was seated on a leaden cloud. He was dismayed to see that though he had gone a good fourteen years before Teru, he was still stuck in his niche. Tabby was afraid that he could remain there forever and be swallowed by those obnoxious and abysmal clouds. Unless, he was prepared to do a re-run of his life and take time out to atone for his black moments. That may buy him a brownie point, but not necessarily the brownies he was so fond of. If Teru too does the same, all this with no spats, no denouncements and no platitudes, it is then possible for the two to keep moving to their divine destination, Tabby supposed and kept his paws crossed.

Grandaunt continuing to engage the children with her fables about the clouds, told them that Grandpa had once made the mistake of harping on the same old grievance of his, of Teru not having got him a dowry. Even before he stopped whining, he had come sliding down to the lower most and the darkest of clouds.

Was that like being swallowed down to the tail by a snake in that board game you taught us to play? I don't at all like the feeling, grumbled the toothless Glen.

Several times he had walked tearfully out of the game when his number ebbed on the board.

Tabby who hadn't liked the times he had lost ground to fellow tabbies over territorial fights said,

Poor boy, I know what you mean.

And there is a way to sort this thing through, said Grandaunt.

The children looked up expectantly. Monday to Wednesday, she said she would jog her memory and get them to network with dear old Grandpa. Thursday to Saturday, she added, they could visit Teru and regale her enough to make her laugh. She hoped that this would help Teru overlook grumpy Grandpa's misdeeds and forgive him. On Sunday, they were to scan the clouds for results.

It was Monday. Grandaunt busied herself cooking a complete meal with pork curry and rice dumplings and the *vermicelli payasam*. Tabby didn't quite care for the menu. Eating the rice dumplings was a messy job as it was an exercise by itself to sink his teeth into the round dumplings which kept rolling in his bowl. To consume the *payasam*, one had to have the deftness with which a Madrasi scooped the floating *rasam* with his fingers. No matter how decorously he tried to savour it, he would always get his whiskers dripping with the sticky syrup which drew the ants to cosy up to him for a lollipop lick.

It smells good Grandaunt. What is the occasion? asked Glen.

It's a Monday, crooned Grandaunt.

And tomorrow is Tuesday, right Grandaunt? said Kenny the enthusiast.

Grandaunt began with her chronicle for Monday. It was a tale about bony Grandpa, which Teru was never tired of recounting to all of mankind. On a visit to a neighbour, Grandpa had been served *chorizo* and he came home smacking his lips and with a mouth full of praise for someone who didn't know the difference between a *vindaloo* and a *bafaath*. The twist in the tale was that Teru had sent the neighbour a bowl of the goodness from her own kitchen. She enjoyed keeping the bony man in the dark and harvested backhanded compliments as her due. Grandpa no doubt relished the food cooked by his wife but only to the extent that he always told her, that the mutton chops served on that or the other occasion was excellent, but not what was on the table before him.

It could do with a something of this or needed a pinch of that, he estimated.

To Teru's exasperation, the encomiums were always in the past tense. The tenor of his culinary assessment, however, remained a constant. After Grandpa was gone, his children provided the subtext to humour Teru.

I saw your old man sniffing the peppered lamb trotters from the window with a scowl on his face.

Have you put in a little of this and a pinch of that? they teased her.

Did someone forget her rudiments? Why is the rice overcooked? Food not fit enough for dogs! they mimicked.

That was when Grandpa's teeth had been strong enough to crack walnuts. Later, when they began to wobble with age, the script changed. He then accused Teru of punishing an old man with rice that was impossible for the grit eating cock to guzzle. Kenny and Glen laughed at his la-di-dah outbursts. What they didn't realize was, he was exercising the rule of thumb to keep the lady bound to the kitchen and keep her out of circulation.

On Tuesday, Grandaunt regaled the children about Grandpa's grim moods. They began with his characteristic monologues,

Where has my this gone...?

or

Will someone find me that ...?

The family had a hard time reading him. If someone got him a razor in place of a pair of tweezers, for all he wanted was to tweeze the overgrown hair sticking out of his right nostril like prickles, or got him a pickaxe instead of a spade, a tongue lashing was to be expected,

You son of a good for nothing toad, monkey's kith, you descendant of a dumb dodo, ... and...

The children didn't quite know who was being berated. Was he kicking himself in the pants or was it meant for them? But they didn't dare to challenge him. These outbursts were followed by occasions when he went into a silent retreat with not a word said for days on end, claimed Grandaunt.

I can vouch for it that his face went dour and he looked murderous, she continued.

On such days, the entire household is supposed to have kept out of his way. And he wasn't even seen talking to the tangy lemon tree with bright orange fruits, as was his habit. A message would then go out to *Mai*, who would make a visit to prepare a bitter concoction out of *sathanache saal*, the bark of a tree whose bitterness was sure to endure beyond Judgment Day. He drank it grudgingly. With that he hung up his mood.

The concoction worked. It brought out an off-the-wall streak in his nature. He laughed, he did. His favourite caricature was of the famed hotelier Rampa of *Kodial*. Anyone visiting Rampa would come away with ideas good enough for an epic burlesque.

The children were told that their grandpa was in splits over Rampa's whimsical gags and watching him laugh, the rest laughed as well. His favourite however, was the one where Rampa had a bout of stomach gripes. The doctor impressed on him the universally acknowledged truth,

Light paarddh jethunda, matha sari aapundu.

He did just that for four days with no end in sight. A revisit to the doctor revealed that Rampa had slept with the lights on, and not with a light tipple as recommended by the doctor. He had taken the doctor's double-edged prescription, literally. Tabby tried to hide his grin by pretending to preen his twitching whiskers at the thought of a tipsy Rampa. And Grandpa never had enough of his gags.

Tabby, Kenny and Glen had never heard of the bony man's winsome ways ever. All the same, the animal biscuits and the coconut taffies he got for his children on his visit to town, and the scarecrows he placed to stand watch in the middle of the green paddy fields endeared the old man to them. He seemed to have made a *gorga* for each of his brood, which made their day. Their only regret was that they couldn't fold it like an umbrella and take it to the city with them. The bamboo rain cover, made of areca palms, with an expanse running up to almost the length of their arms tickled the children's imagination. His children put them on and went along with their father to close or open the water gates on the dykes, unmindful of the wind-driven sheets of drizzle which were heading towards them.

The trio learnt that Grandpa was at his genial best on the Eve of Christmas. That was the only time of the year when his children got to see a huge rum soaked cake he got for his household. He would take it down from behind the altar and cut it ceremoniously, and the children received it with the same reverence as they did the Holy Communion. Though it was Christmas, the children in this household hadn't heard of Santa and of course there were no gifts. Teru's children saw the Santa in Grandpa much after he was gone. They had seen their father sit among his underlings over the Christmas meal and eat the *shoio* with chicken stew laced with coconut milk; the delectable ghee rice topped with mutton chops and *raitha*. The helping hands went home with hampers laden with clothes for their family and sweetmeats and fire crackers for the children.

How could I ever forget the midnight ride in a bullock cart, all the way to the church in the biting cold? echoed Grandaunt.

The sleepy bullocks had to draw the load of the master, his kith and kin, the servants and anyone on the way to the manger. The darkness of the night and the chill literally transported them to Bethlehem. Their journey was incensed by *Raath Ki Raani* in bloom just for the infant and his shepherds under the canopy of a starlit sky.

A night ride in a bullock cart, how romantic, exclaimed Kenny.

That's primitive. I like the family Gypsy. How do you think Aunty Vima would have managed to get into the cart with her bottom that weighed a truck-load, asked the considerate Glen?

They went to bed with no consensus on the issue, but on the matter of Grandpa's generosity, they were unanimous.

This is when Tabby wished to join in to tell them of the time, when Grandpa had taken Aunty Vima, a new bride, to town. He was enamoured by his college educated, fashionable daughter-in-law. He introduced her to the tinker, the butcher, the tailor, the newspaper vendor, the cobbler and the bystanders with the pride of having earned the Coat of Arms. Escorting her home, the bride in her stilettos found the rope walk on the dykes next to impossible and fell into the fields. Completely drenched and not aware that the entire clan was watching her from the hilltop, she chided herself,

This is going to be off the record.

They never let her forget the outing of her lifetime in the company of her bewitched father-in-law.

It was soon Wednesday and Kenny and Glen went looking for their Grandaunt. They found her dressed in her ageless blue floral skirt and an equally worn out pair of canvas shoes. She was leaning on a crook, improvised from a coffee stump.

Grandaunt, where you off to? Remember it is Wednesday? reminded Glen.

I do, I do, I do remember, she said and continued to trek on her way to the plantation.

But, but you promised to tell us..., said an impatient Kenny.

All in good time, you will see, is all that the wistful Grandaunt was prepared to say at that moment.

And they walked on through slope after slope of the green plantations, dizzy with the scent of inviting cherry blossoms, blossoms a bride would covet for a bouquet. Every now and again, Grandaunt stopped to inhale the scent and in yogic contemplation held up a spray of foam-white flowers for inspection. And then began her replay of the rendition by the two, Teru and her bony man of a husband.

Having waited for nine pregnant days after the first blossom shower, your Grandpa was impatient, said Grandaunt.

He went trekking with Teru for company, block after block of the floral terrain. He was delighted at the sight of swarms of drunken bees at work, harvesting nectar from the heady blooms and leaving them with a kiss each. The birds greeted the senior couple with the unrestrained spontaneity of the drunk. He stopped, stared and strolled on with thoughts one couldn't read. Grandpa was known to be abnormally reticent. Soon the density of the blossoms lifted his mood and he imitated a plumed friend calling out to his mate. He then, undid his fly and peed into the undergrowth. Content with the run of the flow or perhaps at the sight of the luxuriant blossoms, he clicked his tongue and said,

Plentiful, plentiful.

A confused Teru, not sure of his intent stood still with her head bent like a question mark. With the sun on the ascent, the two soon returned home, only to resume their trek in the company of friends and a flask of grog, comparing notes. The sun winked his way to the west. The mood prevailed for weeks on end and Teru counted her blessings.

When they could walk no longer, Grandaunt made a U-turn to discover that the two siblings who were quiet for a while were preoccupied with something Grandpa would never have approved of. Kenny's upturned skirt and Glen's pockets were stuffed to the gills with cherry blossoms. Their request,

Grandaunt, will you make us wreaths to put on our heads? went unanswered.

Instead, she hurried them home.

IV

Kindred Meet

It was now going to be Thursday with Teru. The children waited with baited breath to meet their grandmother. When they did, they watched their grandparents, Teru and the bony man explore absolution. But it was like a game of see-saw with neither relenting.

It's a good sign to agree to disagree, a gratified Grandaunt pontificated.

While they ironed out their differences, Grandaunt thought it best to distract the little ones with some more of the old man's lapses not so much to foment Teru's injuries as much as to make her say,

I told you so.

Grandaunt hoped that her brother wouldn't mind being projected as a butt of ridicule if only to assuage Teru's rage and get her to stop sulking and start introspecting. She asked Glen if he remembered Grandpa peeing into the undergrowth. He refused to respond to what he thought was her unusual obsession with excremental stuff. He remembered how she had laughed herself sore talking about the time Grandpa had embarrassed his grandchildren from the city on a visit to the family retreat in Kodagu. As they sauntered down the incline towards a stream on a fishing expedition, they saw their grandpa squatted on a foot bridge easing out long strands of the yellow stuff in public view. Horrified, one of the girls said,

How could he? Gross stuff!

For that was where they had gone looking for crabs the previous weekend. And relished them too.

Two others went keck, keck, keck and bolted from the place. Their father, who had escorted them on their stroll, cleared his throat to sound the old man, but he looked the other way and continued with his job. And there was Grandaunt, his sister, having a go at it once more. A couple of trenches later, she resumed her account of what Grandpa did with a heap of dry leaves piled up in a deliberated mound in a trench.

What do you think it was? she asked them.

Averse to being asked questions, Glen locked horns with her with a counter question,

Why don't you tell us Grandaunt?

At the sight of the pile, Grandpa's nose had begun to flare and twitch, she claimed. He thought that it was the handiwork of Kunchirama who had been caught several times pilfering the ripe coffee berries. He bent over the trench and shuffled the leaves only to sense his fingers sinking into something moist and cold. He pulled back and Teru saw him sniff his fingers to quell his curiosity, as was his habit. In the bargain, he had soiled his nose and his little tooth brush of a moustache. To get rid of the odious thing, he began to towel his hand on his khaki half pants. All of it happened in such reckless haste that Grandpa had no breath left to curse the culprit. Leaving Teru behind, he rushed home to come off the mess. When he emerged from his bath and laundry, he looked kosher clean like Kunjiry Akkavva, only not so coddled.

Akkavva's ritual baths were village famous and the preparation for the same sent everyone about into a tizzy. First the oil massage, then the scrub, followed by rigorous water lashing with the entire cauldron of hot water, the towelling with half a dozen pieces, the hot fermentation of the body, the burning of the scented sandalwood shavings in her room to ward off evil spirits, the pot of soup served at her bedside and finally a nap to seal her day. A luxury Teru could only dream of.

And for unfortunate Grandpa, his blossom-triggered exultant mood was short-lived. For the next couple of days, he was traumatized as word spread of how *Aiyya* had defiled himself and out of season too. Every now and again he was seen sniffing his fingers with a puckered-up nose in abject disapproval of his humiliation.

Even so, he came out of it tall as expected, said Teru to Aaleema.

Of course, with a little help from *Mai* who had her own way of fixing mischief-mongers. Before the cock could crow, she gathered smouldering ash from the fire place and like a *tantric* turned it clockwise thrice around Grandpa's head and made it to the spot. Covering the crap with ash, she spat three mouthfuls over it and with her wrinkled and pinched lips uttered what felt like a string of uncanny vilifications used only by the vulgar,

Rostear podil'lo, … potacho, … hullkot, … chediecho …, papi, … maljauvno, … and spat some more and left the place making sure not to look back.

In three days' time, *Mai's* magic showed how potent it was. The suspect had an inexplicable sore bottom that no quack was willing to look at, gloated Grandaunt.

Kenny and Glen didn't know what to make of it, but agreed that anyone defecating in the open deserved no less, not even Grandpa. At the mention of it, Grandpa perched atop his fizzy cloud appeared to grimace and went sliding down and for the first time the unbending Teru put out her hand to stop his descent.

The children didn't know what to expect when Friday loomed large. They went about picking jasmines for their grandaunt, when she called their attention to a soufflé of clouds gathering in readiness for the much-awaited mango showers. One large and several others of varying mass and hue tread a measure while a remote one with no silver lining stayed put.

That's her, that's her, Grandaunt said in exultation.

Tabby too looked up and saw that Teru was holding forth, changing colour and going up by notches, every now and again with an intentional focus. Though far behind, so did Grandpa.

Was Grandaunt counting her bridges even before she had crossed them? wondered Tabby who was keeping count of the days.

But like Tabby's mistress, Grandaunt was not the one to give up. She curled her fingers on both hands and put them together to make a long enough telescope to view the kaleidoscopic designs in the sky. The children did the same and they smiled at the unpredictable but speaking images.

Grandaunt insisted that Teru was holding centre-stage, narrating to her companion clouds of her visit to Devaraja Urs Market in the company of her man and his wallet. It was a must visit for Teru whenever she happened to be in the once princely city. She couldn't resist the pyramids of *rangoli* colours in the market: the vermillion and the indigo, the saffron and the green, the yellow and the pink dust. Close at hand, were the glass bangle sellers with their riotous ware and she would have loved to have a pick of the green ones speckled with gold. The next segment at the bend greeted her with the gentle aroma of *champaks* and chrysanthemums, jasmines, marigolds and sprays of soothing *tulasi*. The scent lulled her senses and all she wanted to do was of going to bed like a child after a warm bath. The red paraffin bathed pomegranates and the fragrant apples at the fruiterers stretch vying with each other, didn't escape her attention. Most of all, the deep green of the bananas and the purple of the grapes stirred her sensibilities to take in the tapestry of vendors and wares, colours and commotions in their myriad shades.

I wish he'd let me have the mouth-watering mix of the crunchy copra chips with candy sugar, jaggery, roasted sesame and peanuts and an occasional almond in hiding? she drooled.

If only the vendors kept out of their way with their, '*Sarey, Sarey, ...,*' perhaps she would have managed to draw his attention to the assorted delicacy.

Her musings were abruptly shattered and replaced by the picture of her husband with a coconut in hand ready to smash a vendor's skull to smithereens. Grandpa not having obliged this vendor with a visit to his stall, found the 'Sarey' subtly turned to a '*Suarey*'. He was not willing to be called a swine by a .... and be sworn at. How was the vendor expected to know that this man of hers could speak seven languages effortlessly?

Teru was in awe of his courage to stand up in a situation of the kind. The motley Dussehra crowd stood still to watch how the squabble would pan out. The setting too was in disarray. The mutiny of colours and a sea of people kept mixing and churning themselves out forming a pattern to no avail. Some women dressed in blue saris with yellow underskirts showing, mismatched with turkey-red blouses were the show-stoppers. Their braids were so taut that the tip ends were raised like the waving hood of a cobra, having been fastened to hold it in place with an emerald green ribbon. The rest of the throng enhanced the psychedelic scene. And their menfolk matched them in their festive madness, measure for measure. The colour of their shirts ranged from a crimson red to a sunflower yellow to a peroxide blue. Their folded lungis with their striped chaddies showing was a sheer case of Sundays being longer than Mondays. And their enthusiasm for a glimpse of the glittering goddess Chamundi on the howdah and their King, the Jayachamarajendra Wodeyar was unmistaken. On this day, the celebratory crowd was in no state of mind to take sides between the accosted and the accuser. It was a disappointing day for Teru.

Tabby was distracted by what seemed to be a celestial build up towards a climax. The assembly around Teru was getting bigger, and it was a Saturday. Tabby spotted the bony man on the outer ring, evincing great interest in the goings on with an occasional smile. He no longer looked pallid.

Good for him, crooned chirpy Glen.

Subsequently, Glen went about chasing a surge of dragon flies emerging from the earth. When he did manage to catch one, he asked his grandaunt to loop its wings so that he could remote fly the creature at will. Tabby disapproved of his ill-chosen gratification, though he would have liked to snack on a couple of them for want of anything better to do. Instead, he looked the other way and began to clamber his way up a tree.

About that time, Tabby saw a flurry of movement in the firmament. One of the remote clouds had built up its own constellation, cloud for cloud with Teru pedestal centred. What bewildered him was the switching of sides by those peripheral clouds. Kommethodu Lucy who had all along kept company with Teru, was seen sneaking off to the bony man's camp. Her reason, while Teru had been good to her, it was her spouse who supported her nomination to head the panchayat. He had campaigned tooth and nail to ensure that the marginalized had a chance to lead from the front. Tabby recognized Chella and his wife Chellathi, who were obliged to *Aiyya* for the tenancy rights the old man had helped them secure. Grandpa had an entire community of Gandhi's own men, the *Harijans* and the *Girijans* rallying around him. They said,

If our kith down there are bankers and teachers, we owe it to him.

A Gandhian, *Aiyya* had ensured that their children went to school.

Among the fence-sitter clouds were Aaleema to whom the master and the mistress were an inseparable entity. She had agonized over their travails, laboured with Teru over the delivery of a dozen babies and they in turn had reciprocated generously in times of plenty. Aaleema's soap nut vending father Alira Mammunchi Maestry was a small-time trader. He leased orchards after orchards of orange even before the blooms could show up.

He placed hefty bouncers with bows and a quiver laden with arrows to walk among the orange-heavy orchards, to keep off the light-fingered filchers and ravens, with a vociferous *yoo-hoo*. Several times in a day, they beat on empty oil tins suspended from tree-tops to scare away the thieving crows and monkeys. The clang, rang through the hills and dales. But here, Maestry was seen bridging the distance between the two cliques. And when he saw Beppunadu Bosthu, the one with the limp join them, Maestry bared his toothless gums in a welcome grin. So, did the bony man. Tabby's whiskers stood ramrod straight at the turn of events.

Bosthu comes from *Mai's* village, said Teru as an introduction to her side of the faction. And he was the bony man's buddy in their youth.

The bony man vouched for it that Bosthu was an extraordinary kid and there was no other like him when it came to his flair for flatus. He could break wind effortlessly and at will. Walking back from school, the kids from the village would often challenge Bosthu to a losing wager. Bosthu would fling his school bag to one side, go down on fours, raise his bottom and call out,

Ready, steady and here I go!

The boys got as close to his rumps as they dared to and counted,

One, two, three, ..., nine, ..., fifteen, ..., and gave up.

119

There were too many of them and some were brazenly loud, a few gusty enough to kick up a sandstorm in the Sahara, and the others subdued and weak. The bony man and his companions tickled by the range, rolled on the ground, roared with laughter, punched each other till they got breathless and then in unison, they implored Bosthu to stop.

How could he? He could always start at will, but stop he couldn't, till he had run the full course, claimed Teru with gusto, engaging her brood with tales of yore.

Her companion clouds chortled, tickled by Bosthu's bold stroke and bounced up and up, quite as Teru's children did in the days gone by around the grinding stone.

When Bosthu was a little under ten, a time when the Gandhian leach pits hadn't yet reached Beppunaadu, he took great delight in crawling up a fallen tree trunk to do his job. As always, he couldn't start the job unless he fired a volley of thunderous shots and then he would finish the task in one great whoosh! Sanvanda Manu, a Kodava, walking to his farm with a double barrel gun on his shoulders, heard some unearthly sounds like those made by the *koolies,* the local spirits in distress. To drive them out of the vicinity, he aimed a shot. No *Koolie* but Bostu was caught in the crossfire. His hip went kaput and Bosthu continued to limp for the rest of his life.

The story doesn't end there, said Teru to her children who never took responsibility for accidents that happened at the other end of their anatomy, ever. She swore by the grinding stone that, Bosthu's kinsfolk never let him forget his brush with death either and nicknamed him Boom Boom Bosthu.

Teru had a premonition that Bosthu's presence would felicitate the union between her and the bony man, his friend.

A newly forming middle order headed by Maestry and Bosthu, began to get bigger and with that the leftists and the right winged forces were drawn in, as is the nature of a cloud, albeit resisting the merger with thunderous uproar. But by sunset, the calibrated effort had paid off. Tabby noticed that their differences were getting smaller and nonconformity was no longer an issue, all except one.

The legion of clouds recognized the brooding bride, Manjula Waddar from the stone cutter's quarry from Hubli, the one who had been chopped to pieces by her husband, before he turned himself in. And all for embarrassing him before his family and friends with a smelly *uuusss* that escaped from her with a toot while she was serving them her first presentation meal. Her body was bent from waist down over the banana leaves laid out on rectangular platforms on the floor, at a luncheon customarily prepared by a bride at her spouses' house to greet her new relatives. It was apparent that the lady was meant to rot in her present disposition as her remorseless husband continued to be embarrassed despite the thirty years he served behind bars and a dog's death he died in a public lavatory soon after. A search for him among the clouds went in vain. The remorseless one was nowhere to be seen, not even after a lapse of four decades.

Was he lost behind the monstrous black clouds? wondered the sorry souls.

Barring that, the place was filled with distinct bands of souls. Tabby witnessed large soul-chains like the colourful but winged Warli dancers decking the outermost reaches of the horizon.

A thought crossed Tabby's mind:

Is Grandaunt spinning fanciful stories to keep the children engaged or is she passing on a tradition of beliefs to the generations after her?

It was hard for him to accept that he no longer had Teru to validate Grandaunt's claims.

It was Jerusalem Sunday. A day when everyone met everyone at church in their Sunday best. Tabby surprised himself by asking,

Isn't Jerusalem also the heavenly abode of the blessed?

Either no one heard him or they ignored him as cats always are wont to. Let down, he moved to the cemetery to look for Teru. The family followed him to attend Teru's funeral- mind service. It stood around the red mound of earth looking grim. For some reason, he couldn't read their minds as he did when Teru was around in her supernatural status. Her resting place was once again showered with a rain of flowers and a shocking sprinkle of holy water from a cruet. The spray transported him out of the world of the dead to the world of the living, back to the funeral home where Kenny and Glen stood crossing SUNDAY with a red marker on the calendar.

So, Sunday it is, meowed Tabby and jumped off the *aimara* to scan the firmament for one last time.

It was serene and cloudless. He wondered what Grandaunt was going to make of it when she stepped out with the children at twilight.

Hopping back on to his sun-bathed seat on the sill, he caught himself eyeballing the mirror, screening a spectrum of colours. The likes of which he had never seen in his lifetime of thirteen years. Enthralled, he scanned the moving pictures in the inner world of the mirror and saw the flaming orange sun being escorted by clusters of bah bah woolly clouds, the kind that graze on the Scottish pastures. The soft clusters were now down- feather- white, now daffodil yellow, now turning salmon pink. As the sun dipped, Tabby saw the sky draped in orange stripes interspersed with bands of purple.

Here's another Spirit Pageant, but bereft of the celestial cast, he reflected bewildered.

He then asked,

Where have all the dear departed gone?

Looking for an answer he made a dash to Grandaunt's side of the quarter to check how she would spell out the development.

Shading her eyes with the palms of both her hands, he heard her say with incomprehension writ large on her face,

Well, …?

Kenny and Glen, went ditto and asked in unison,

Well...?

An agitated and expectant Tabby with a stiff tail broke in,

Well, …?

FOREWORD

The other woman, …

She lives on. She is ninety-four and holding on. Just as well you might say.

If she were to die, will she navigate through 'after life' like Teru did?

It's your word as against mine for this other woman is Awra!

So there.

Why, you do not even know what will happen tomorrow. What is your life? You are a mist that appears for a little while and then vanishes.

James 4:14

PART II

Not Everyone Dies

Chapter 5

LIVING IN THE LAYERS

I

Leaving Footprints

Awra lives.

She was christened Aurelia Remedia Esperancia Garcia. She lives on the Konkan coast, miles away from Teru. At ninety-four, she is in no hurry to meet the Reverend.

I'm not done with life yet, she insists.

I am sure to like the tomorrows better than my todays, she affirms.

But for all the unpredictability of the tomorrows, Awra's todays are regimented.

At a meal, a red fish curry accompanied by the red beetroot salad and the *thambdi bajji,* also red, does not appeal to her visual appetite. A rainbow spread of a turmeric tinged fish curry, a green *subji* and a tri-coloured salad were more like it. For reasons, best known to her, her bathing regimen was determined in consultation with the position of the moon and the stars. She would not wash her hair on a new or a full moon day. In contrast, her day-to-day conventions were a constant.

They better look the same, feel the same and smell the same or they ran the risk of being suspect, claimed Chibby.

Chibby, her ally was accustomed to Awra's heuristic ways. Stillness among the trees would make her look grim as she expected a tsunami to trounce the wicked in some part of the world; an orange sky was certain to bring in an abundance of pink perches, Awra predicted. Chibby liked it that way as she knew what to expect of her mistress on any given day.

Tabby admired Awra's Chibby for her composure and courted her to be the mother of his kittens. He made a good husband and was chivalrous to her always. For fear of displeasing Chibby, he was attentive to her tales about Awra and her household. To her it was always Awra over Teru. It didn't matter if he had his own take on the issue. This prompted him to tell his kittens,

Learn from me, never cross a lady lest you should live to rue the day.

Leaving Teru to her destiny, Tabby had eventually returned to his hearth and home. Unusually, it didn't quite feel the same anymore. He spent his time brooding and occasionally looking over the wall to catch a glimpse of Chibby who lived four houses away from him. When he saw her dozing on Awra's lap, he missed Teru's company. A couple of days later, she saw him sitting on the compound wall sulking. Chibby took him to task,

C'mon Tabby, be a man, snap out of it. Learn from Awra.

Chibby went on to tell him of the day when the tragic news of a daughter's death was broken to Awra. She had squeezed herself in the space between the wall and the refrigerator in the corner of the dining place and wept bitterly from dawn to the setting of the sun. When she came out of the corner, she had resolved to put it behind her. Whereas her husband, the man with the whistle in his lungs, succumbed to grief.

Be a man, be a man, she exhorted.

Saying so, Chibby fondly brushed her curvaceous body against his, jumped off the wall and left. Back home, she had half a dozen kittens waiting to be nursed.

Chibby was grateful to Awra for having seen her through a gruelling labour the previous time. Writhing in pain, Chibby had gone to her. She was picked up tenderly, placed on her lap and given a reassuring massage on her long silken, but taut back. When it was about time, Chibby braced herself for the act. She stood tall and thrust her head into Awra's arm pit and whelped, six kittens, one at a time. And Awra didn't once flinch.

That's what you call a tough act which comes from living with the tough, said Chibby taking pride in her mistress.

Awra had gathered her lessons the hard way. Life is full of them and they visit only the chosen. She was among the jinxed. The toughest of them all was living in poverty which tempered her like steel. She was a child of the wartimes, born seventeen years after her only sibling. And she lost her father soon after. The only memory she had of him was of getting spanked with a wiry twig, swish, swish, swish, all for having done a good deed. She had let her neighbour know, that her papa had poisoned her mother hen and her brood of chicks who scratched around in his garden, uprooting the tender bean saplings.

On several occasions, Chibby had heard Awra live through the events of that day.

It was quite like World War I, only instead of muskets at work the two neighbours exchanged acerbic abuses. The mourners called the killer a dipsomaniac, a *bebdo*, a wife-basher, which he was, and a *malcriado*, a *papi*. The blue-eyed killer turned angry-red and reciprocated with acrimony. He called the lady a cantankerous offspring of a toddy-tapper, a *surantt*.

When they had run out of ammunition, they retreated. And then began the inquisition at home. Awra's mother came out in flying colours. She took care to see that she didn't step out of line of her alcoholic husband's dressing-down, for fear of being made to walk round and round the *taluka* till she almost dropped dead. He often bawled at her for transgressions on her part,

Keep walking you widow wife, keep walking till your back crumbles.

But did Awra? Her father put the three-year-old on his lap and tried to wring the truth out of her. He sweet-talked her,

How did the neighbours know that I have done what they claim I have done?

Affection failed, bribing yielded no result, veiled threats in the name of Beelzebub didn't work. And then out came the twig and the neighbour heard a swish, swish, swish. Those alabaster white legs and her naked back displayed a tapestry of marbled streaks, of purple, green and red for the next fortnight. But Awra was tight lipped and at every stage she only said,

Tem, tem, tem- that, that, that, in her high-pitched voice, choking occasionally and no more.

Afraid, she was not. Mission aborted, but Awra had earned a value. She told Chibby,

Never let the one with his hand in the cookie jar score over you.

Tabby almost said,

She is quite like the iron willed Teru, but held his own as he didn't wish to be party to yet another squabble.

A cold-war ensued between the neighbours. Awra, not in league with either, chose to do what she thought was right. As usual, when her nostrils tingled with the wind-borne aroma of the fish curry in vinegar, she picked up her white enamelled bowl with the blue rim, and walked across to her neighbour to grade their curry. They filled her bowl to the brim, in exchange for transactions under her roof. Awra, had hitherto, was known to have prattled on, often indiscreetly. But after the swish, she was not prepared to sell out her papa and the neighbour decided to hit back. The following day, the bowl was filled to the brim, with no questions asked. Awra sitting astride on the high threshold of her house savoured the finger licking curry. It took but minutes five, her stomach began to heave and soon she was choking for breath from the surging pools of acidic vomit. Once again, her papa tried to get to the root of the matter, with nothing forthcoming. Years later, Awra was told by the same neighbour that her curry had been laced with an herbal concoction to break her greed.

Did it? asked Tabby with a casual air while preening his whiskers from the roots to its pointed tip.

For one thing, it did stop Awra from visiting the neighbours with her bowl. Tabby often thought that her interest in food was beyond normal. Not wanting to score a self-goal by acquiescing to his remark, Chibby ignored him. To Awra food was a creature comfort and it was none of Tabby's business to keep an eye on who ate what and how much, she told herself.

Guesstimating what was on her mind, Tabby decided to humour her. He asked,

Every time the fish comes riding home on the Malabari's bicycle, why's that Awra's thumb runs behind her fore-finger, over the length of the fish, like a green maggot walking the span of the tender French beans?

A slight smile was seen flitting over Chibby's face at the analogy, yet, she decided to keep a stiff upper lip and not let Tabby know that Awra was measuring the length of the fish to calculate how many servings it would make. Besides, she was not going to be the one to remind Tabby that each of Awra's curried fish pieces were accurate in size not exceeding two inches anytime.

And why does she open the flap over the gill of each fish and get close to them as if she had a hush- hush message to share with them? asked the cheeky Tabby.

Well, that is what I call a close encounter, Chibby tried to shut him up with a veiled threat.

Or was she asking the fish if she was willing to drop in at her kitchen for a cup of tea? he retorted twitching his whiskers in a trice.

Those limp little cuttlefish, why did she heave and retch at the sight of them? intoned Tabby to Chibby's exasperation.

Chibby decided to circumvent his observations and began to doze off. But when Tabby saw a goal in sight, he wasn't the kind to give up. He went on,

How's that when it came to the cuttle's twice removed crustacean cousins, the crabs, she would have her lanky husband crack them with his teeth to help her extract their pound of flesh?

Do you remember the day when she told her grandchildren that the Chinese are full of tape worms to dissuade them from chomping noodles? he persevered.

Chibby decided that enough was enough and snapped,

I think the same too, the way they slurp noodles morning, noon and night.

Well, I can see that Awra no longer desists from eating noodles. In fact, I love to see her swallow the serpentine strands in one long swoosh! Tabby said sucking in air in imitation of Awra.

Suppressing her amusement, Chibby simply said,

If only you realized what it means to grow up with an empty feeling in the pit of your stomach. For such of them life is a long wait for showers of opportunities.

II

Throes of Hunger

Life was painful for a daughter being raised by a single parent in the post-war period with a father long dead. Awra didn't complain of hunger or want of comforts. She lived in London *vaddo*, where the affluent lived. She took delight in watching the privileged English speaking girls of her age go to church in a horse- drawn carriage dressed in fine silk. The Kabuliwalah brought the gossamer fabric from beyond the Pass and sold it from door to door. All Awra asked for were two favours: a veil when she came of age like the one Praxis covered her head with and the man who wished to marry her to provide for her mother as well.

That isn't a tall order, is it? asked Chibby to no one.

Awra came of age, and mother went without a meal or two to get her the veil. Time went by and men knocked at her door to ask for her hand, but none so noble in answer to her prayer. And mother chose to die before her time, so Awra could live. Since then, Awra has had no expectations, but only the resolve to live on without despairing.

All the same, Awra cherished her childhood and never gave up reminiscing about it. Watching Chibby sleep for long hours with her kittens, Awra was reminded of the day when she told her mother,

Mama, stay in bed a tad longer. I want to sleep on, with you by my side.

A foolish mother gave into the pleas of a more foolish daughter and both slept on till the sun was over their heads. At noonday, the girl woke up to a ravenous wolf growling in her stomach and tears rolling down her face. She couldn't fight hunger and learnt that love didn't always come with a bunch of roses, but with a price tag on its shoulders.

Eventually, Awra fell in love with an almost penniless, but a good man. Unlike Teru's husband who complained that she brought him no dowry, here was Awra with a princely sum of Rs. 2,500/- that had been squirreled away from her father's salary, a little at a time, by his employer and bishop who was a twice removed cousin of his. Endearingly, the minister called the girl *Bai* and she liked the *nom de plume*. On her fortnightly visit to the bishop's house to collect her allowance, some of his utility men received this comely girl with cheer and asked her for her name and ledger number. She cocked her head to let everyone about know that it was *Bai*.

Oh, no, not that, but your real name, insisted the simpleton behind the desk to be told by her that her name was indeed *'Bai'*, B-A-I - *Bai* and no other.

Thereafter, whenever they had the privilege of meeting her, in unison they chorused,

Here comes our B-A-I- *Bai*.

And they did it with such aplomb that Awra began to suspect their credentials. Soon she discovered that the privilege of being called *Bai* was reserved for the chosen few and that she was indeed Aurelia Remedia Garcia Esperancia and would remain so. But her young memory playing truant at having to parrot the long line of those Latinate names, in the order in which they were given to her, she chose to reinvent herself. In no uncertain terms, she told the bearded Bishop, her grand uncle,

Bappu, you will call me by my Christian name, I mean my new name and no other, won't you?

141

And that settled it. She rechristened herself Grace.

What a far cry from those Latinate names which were more than a mouthful, Tabby cried out.

Chibby chipped in to say that she has never known her by any other name to this day. Those baptismal names turned up when Babutti was updating the family record in the Bible after the demise of his father. Awra turned red when her furtive list of names became common knowledge.

In retrospect, Awra recalled having grown wary of such tags as *Bai* as she was full of yarns of people in her community who had been branded with names that couldn't be shed for love or money. One such was her immediate childhood neighbour who was a chronic bachelor. Not having found a suitable bride to compliment his social status as a *bamonn* and match his big- headed temperament, he did something that no subject dared to do. He looked overseas. He wrote,

My Good Queen Bess,

I'm your very subject, and I've a proposition to make. But before I do that, let me bare myself. I've no crown to offer you, but all I have is yours, my Virgin Queen, to use as you will. And it isn't much in terms of worldly standards. I've twelve other siblings and a widowed mother who will be honoured if you accept my hand in marriage, as it will improve her prospects and put an end to your painful single-hood.

If you wish to know why it is that I have not chosen to marry one of my kind, let me tell you that they do not have your verve. I admire the fervour with which you swear at those bishops. I hold dear your pluck at having thrown your shoes at the heads of the diplomats. Oh, how I cherish the way you boxed the ears of the Earl of Essex. And you need no longer dance the whole night to dodge the likes of the Spanish Ambassador. You will Gloriana, my Majesty, be truly happy in my company, as I am well versed in all the tricks you use and I assure you, you will be quite at home and can be yourself always.

I'm serious in my intent and I await your royal response. Please say aye to my proposal of marriage.

Yours in hope,
Bob

And Bob dropped the letter into the wall mounted red letter box at Kodialbail with the royal cipher *G.R.* inscribed on it. Returning home with a sigh of relief he waited. In a fortnight's time, a platoon of bobbies knocked on his door with a warrant bearing the royal insignia for his arrest, only to discover that our groom had gone slightly loony from having waited endlessly to walk up the aisle. It was apparent that the bloke was stranded between the ages and couldn't tell the difference between one and the other of the Elizabeths. A prompt report was dashed off by the English cops to the incumbent George VI. He had the grace not to take umbrage at so weird a proposal that was behind schedule, to some royal kin. And his daughter, Elizabeth II, the princess presumptive was amused.

Awra told herself,

Love is not just blind, it's dumb as well. Look what it did to Bob, divesting him of his given name.

Subsequently, he came to be known as *'Rani Ganda'*, Queen's Husband. He became the butt of many a joke and kept his large family and ruthless community regaled. About the time, it was also rumoured that a certain grand Duchess of a lesser kingdom in Europe was widowed and the same neighbourhood lost no time in suggesting to the younger brother of the disappointed groom that he could now send her an offer of marriage. His sanity intact, he chose to ignore them, but couldn't fight the name they dubbed him with. They called him, *'Munde Ganda'*, Widow Husband. And the name stuck. Awra was wary of such cruelty visiting mankind and she wished to steer clear of its ambit. The feline commentators of human foibles didn't approve of such names either.

Point being taken, the Bishop, her *Bappu*, conceded to her request and Awra became Grace from that day forth, with care taken to shelve her baptismal names from posterity.

Awra had similar other codices added to her repertoire of do's and don'ts. One among them was,

Don't forget your antecedents. Your rootedness will forge your identity, she told herself.

She recalled that she was named Aurelia for *Domus Aurea*, 'The House of Gold,' so precious was her birth. The thought sustained her during trying times, when she was left with neither an abode nor gold.

And her father liquidated the gold in the house to celebrate her birth, didn't he? asked Tabby.

On the other hand, Teru's father, had to undersell *Mai's* gold to foot the medical bills of their only son. That boy was sick for as long as the chest held gold in it, so it was said, reported Tabby.

The women didn't complain. It was not their place to do so. But Aurelia was among a breed of her own and she took charge of her life by withdrawing this name from public domain. She hated to have her name sullied. Folks called her 'Auwra' which wasn't bad except that they used it as a slur to remind her of the ill-omened day she was born on. The 1923 deluge left her house and those of the people of London *vaddo* entirely submerged. '*Auwr*' in her native tongue meant floods, a devastative association and therefore the revulsion for the name. That she didn't possess an ounce of gold to redeem her name only furthered her resolve to re-christian herself as Grace.

Just as well, I can't stand talk of floods, substantiated Tabby.

Among some of Tabby's other not so favourite things were his utter dislike of mankind's prudery. Watching Awra's clothes on the line, Tabby was befuddled and had asked Chibby,

Why would you want to wear layers and layers of clothes? Never have I seen an elephant or an ant don a shirt on his back or an under-pant for that matter.

At times, Chibby detested Tabby's bent of mind and she snorted. The subject was sure to have heckled Awra, she thought. Heckled she was by a rich aunt. Without notice, she had lifted Awra's humble dress to see whether she had on her lingerie. To a girl of twelve, it was mortifying. Let down by poverty, Awra was deprived of such unmentionables. Thereafter, Awra had refused to visit this aunt in health and in sickness and her mother couldn't fathom why.

Modesty is dear to the poor as well, announced Chibby and crossed herself and made a wish to shoo away penury from ever visiting Awra.

Amen, said Tabby as expected of him.

Tabby was appreciative of certain attributes of Awra. Her determination and fundamental devotion to marriage mystified him. He said,

I must give the devil her due. I like her gumption for the way she honoured her commitment to her spouse and the family she was married into.

Having lost her parents early in life, she pleaded with her brother,

Dattu make sure to be home on the big day and escort me to the altar.

When he failed to respond, she did two things no other bride would have thought of: she bought him not only his ticket to get home but also 'the honour gift, the *Dharma Sado*,' the last of them coming from a bride's parental home; and a couple of days after her betrothal, she threw her humble trousseau into a wicker basket and moved it to her new home after dusk, this time to save the honour of the family she was joining and to avoid tongues from wagging. The move was so unlike the ones among brides who were accompanied by the Hope Chest made of rosewood, boxes that marked their status, a gift given to the bride by her parents, that was cherished for a lifetime and sometimes passed on from mother to daughter. Awra did without the customary entourage accompanying a bride to her new home, to see her off as a matter of tradition, to ensure that she had a past where she belonged. Awra was grateful to her new family for their unconditional acceptance of her without as much as a word said or looks cast beyond her shoulders in expectation of family in attendance. It taught her to forgive herself and accept the lessons poverty had foisted on her.

Poverty is a cruel teacher. By about five, Awra had begun to sweat it out for the family, to keep the fire burning. When her mother couldn't spare as much as an *anna* to buy sardines or prawns that were available aplenty, she would go along with her brother to the water-logged fields in the monsoons, bearing an Indian lantern in one hand and in the other a *chembu* suspended at the neck with a coir rope. She rolled up her dress and waded through the fields in search of the slippery black trout that came in along the muddy and rain-fed streams. Her brother knifed them one at a time and dropped them into the brass *chembu*. It was only a seasonal feast.

Likewise, soon after harvest, came the stately looking flock of cranes to feed on the fallen grains. They would line up on the dykes preening their pristine white wings, stretching them along their pink legs. They resembled the feathered ladies at The Royal Ascot. *Dattu* would aim his gun at them. A couple of them at one shot would ensure that Awra and her family had plenty to feed on for the next couple of days. So too, the birds that found their way into the cooking pot, all for having visited Awra's backyard to savour the wild figs. In times of plenty, Awra had her fill. At others, she learnt to live with less.

When it came to Awra's reasoning, there was a congenital fault with her matrix. It was beyond anyone to count the number of pieces of chicken or fish in floating gravy. But Awra did, before, and after the meal, remembering also to keep an eye on the depleting numbers in the pot as they were being served. An older dependent wondered what it was that Awra did to the fish that he couldn't tell whether it was a sardine or a mackerel that he was served, or lamb or cockerel stew. The gravy in his plate ran all over, the coffee in his mug had no strength. No one had the heart to tell him that her indwelling spirit was so small that she couldn't bring herself to give.

Chibby was embarrassed to hear neighbours gossip. One of them belched like an angry truck,

Why does she do a thing like that? Driving the elderly dependent to our doorsteps for a bowl of zestful curry to kick-start his flattened taste buds, having recovered from a bout of flu, it's a shame.

On her husband's funeral day, his remains laid out for public viewing, Awra lost her decorum once again, visiting the kitchen ever so often to keep tab on the food sent by a condoling neighbour. She couldn't take her eyes off the wedges of fish immersed in the gravy.

But age is a great leveller. It puts one through the wringer so you may complete your education here, though late in the day. At ninety, Job's disease has hit her. She itches with hives, thick as thickets, having broken all over her body with the result that she has had to give up foods ranging from pork to lamb, cock to cockles and shrimps to spinach. And more: bottles of soft creamy cheese spread, having over lived their shelf life, some half used with blue fungal plants growing in them, camouflaged with layers of wrap to conceal them from drawing attention, others intact, hidden in her wardrobe; pitted dates with vermin feasting on them; variety of wheat crackers and soup cubes, nuts and toblorones. Awra had it all surreptitiously for fear of having to share it with the rest. Jobs itch necessitated Awra to chuck her stock, which she did, learning that anything not shared, tastes like ash.

Often Chibby had heard Awra rue to the tune of,

With Job, God went too far to have him prove his allegiance to Him.

Who could tell what Awra's maker wanted of her? reflected Tabby.

III

Sage-ness of a Mother

Awra's love for her children was skewed. There was a role reversal. A mother that she is, she preferred to be a daughter instead.

That sounds like a riddle, countered Tabby with a creased forehead.

For Awra, her daughter's birth was like the breaking-in of a young colt. At seven months of pregnancy, Awra was seen off to her maternal aunt's home 'Bethel' for postpartum care. She left her spouse's home decked in a salmon- pink silk sari, gifted by her husband, glass bangles for good omen and a head weighed down by jasmines and *abolim* from their own backyard and an extravaganza of ignorance. She was told by women who adorned her, that in a while from then, like all lactating mothers, she would have to keep off jasmines to have milk flowing.

At 'Bethel', she was received warmly by more women and a feast. But Awra kept away from these women as she was ill at ease. She sensed stickiness trickling down her legs with no undergarment to hold it back. Confused, she tried to stop it with her legs drawn close. She confined herself to the coconut grove taking care not to take a seat. She avoided company and the love of her life, food. Two hours went by and an older aunt cornered her to figure out why Awra wasn't being receptive. Like Karna who put up with the sting worm boring into his thigh so as not to disturb his guru who was reclining on his lap, here was Awra in premature labour without as much as a whimper having escaped her lips, for fear of embarrassing herself before other women.

Chibby couldn't praise Awra enough for her spirit of endurance and her dauntless approach in confronting crisis.

The women took charge and moved her into a makeshift labour room in the house as home deliveries were the order of the day. Sixteen hours later, her first-born appeared with a long egg-shaped head. The *kathri* birth had taken its toll on Awra and she didn't care what the result was. But the event, catapulted Awra from being a damsel to a dame. The humiliation of a birth of having to sit astride face-to-face on the lap of a stranger with her legs straddled around his torso, and nearly frothing in the mouth, helped in the breaking in. The women who had seen the transformation alleged so.

To Awra's relief, her daughter took charge of her for the next fifty-three years. There on, one not so fine a day of that year, as all mothers' ought to go before their children, this daughter who had been mother, took leave. For the second time, life dealt a blow and Awra couldn't figure out, 'Why?' She tackled her bitterness by stating,

I suppose my daughter like my mother has gone on a date with death.

For all the trauma of birth, the second child arrived soon after. Young Awra had no way of fending off the advances of an eager husband. Unlike Awra's feisty first born, who hogged all the attention, this other child neither became a mother, nor a daughter. In a struggle for survival, she lived from one day to the next. A year later, she was side-stepped further with the arrival of a boy, an occasion for celebration in Indian homes. But with the World War looming large, and Depression staring everybody in the face, Babutti was described as the ominous one, responsible for the War and the recession. He was made to bear the brunt of being born at such a time.

Or why would anyone have him walk to school when his post-war sibling had a joy ride by the school bus?

Is that why Babutti had his meals in the school at the common refectory and his brother at the Rector's corner with soup and dessert for accompaniment? asked Tabby.

When Babutti grew up, he asked everybody around,

Do I find a mention in history for my contribution to the War?

There was a lull for the duration of the war and the cradle stopped rocking for a while. Hitler did himself in, and the next addition to the family had timed his arrival. Peace and prosperity descended on Awra and the world at large. The destiny of a child is in the hands of war-weary parents thought the older boy as he saw Awra cherishing the infant who grew to be a boy and then a man in fine fettle.

Children don't choose their parents, and parents get distanced from one or the other of their children by instinct, mumbled Chibby in defence of her mistress.

I don't understand. Did that happen to you? quizzed Tabby.

Chibby dodged the question with the story of Pattachi, the family cow, whom she had seen butting her calf of two to keep her away from her freshly swelling udders. She had witnessed a pigeon pair pecking and clawing at the winged toddlers to evict them from their parental nest in readiness for the arrival of the new batch of fledglings. Unlike the birds and beasts of nature, when the time came for Awra to wean the favoured one, she refused and nurtured him over the others. Quite like Rebecca did, Awra reserved the Biblical blessing in favour of the younger, ignoring the tradition prevalent among her people. By the same quirk in her nature, she also put the little women, her daughters, above her sons. And then to make sure she would have it her way in old age, she stealthily made a trip to the astrologer to have her destiny mapped out for her.

She asked the man with the decorated forehead, with a vermilion dot on a band of ash, an all-important question,

Will the fine fettled one, be my succour in old age?

The astrologer studied the lines on her palm, tossed the cowrie shells on a grid marked with outlandish symbols and made his calculations from a chart and in the manner of the oracles stated,

The rejected will accept you and no other.

Babutti had no place in her future just as he didn't feature in her past. To debunk the man's muddled predictions, she told herself repeatedly,

This is downright hogwash, and walked away defying destiny.

Awra was surely yoked by something that nobody could put a finger on. Yet she was happy among her younglings when they were with her. Chibby vouched for it. But when her daughters and sons grew out of pigtails and graduated to long pants, they said not a word but stared at some of her ways, baffled.

Awra got them to kneel and confess their sins and shortcomings before the Sunday service, Chibby said embarrassed.

Mama *Padre*, I've sinned. I am the one who stole the *chaklis*, said her much-loved son.

Tell me how my son, so that I may ask Jesu to pardon you.

Well, Mama, when you were fending off Babutti's hugs and kisses, I pirated the bunch of keys from your pocket and passed it on to 'the glow worm', the daughter- mother, who got us the *chaklies* from the jar in the shelf.

The backlash that followed in the next couple of days made the children, who were unwittingly pitted against each other, wary of her ways. Thereafter, they checkmated her with a standard list of transgressions to stop her from causing calculated dissension among the siblings.

The fine-fettled one, try as he did, could never disremember the routine recital of the daily rosary and the knocks he received on the head for dozing off through the five decades as many times. He simply asked, what on earth makes you repeat the same prayer a thousand times and towards what end? He was certain that the dependant elder's endless Hail Mary's over and above the decade were intentional to chastise the children for their apathy towards prayers and the recital of the rosary itself. On such days, the drowsy boy looked at his mother and asked,

How could he go on and on? Mom be sure to cut short the rosary by a decade or two.

When reprimanded for his interruptions, he would further say,

Don't you realise how hectic a day I've had. I've been to school, done my copy-writing, I've had to fight with Martin to get him to work out my sums, and I've had to play as well. Just look at my eyes, they can no longer see.

To add to her woes, at dinner Babutti the bold, cornered her. He asked,

Mama, how's that he has two pieces each of chicken and potato in his plate while I have only one of each in mine?

With no notice, a bowl came flying in his direction. Babutti being Babutti, agile and athletic ducked and the bowl crashed against the neatly stacked pieces of crockery on a rack against the wall. In a domino effect, the glasses and bowls came tumbling down to the accompaniment of their own music with amplified high-fidelity razor-sharp clinks. Chibby and Tabby waiting patiently under the table to pick up scraps after the children, screeched and took to their paws. The children at the table thrust their fingers in their ears and screamed petrified. Awra stood still in a rage and Babutti deliberated over his lucky escape.

But episodes of the kind didn't stop him from speaking his mind. On another occasion, he asked,

Can anyone tell me why I get the crust-end slices of bread day after day?

Because you are an 'Endian,' Awra muttered under her breath.

He didn't quite understand the context until he saw her at the school office in the company of Mr. Kanute, the head teacher, the following day. Awra wanted the boy detained in class three to break his spirit. Mr. Kanute had parents who left a crowing rooster under his table or a dozen *mundappas* to placate him to get their thick-skulled wards to the higher class. But this one with her head inclined to one side and a bewitching smile to go with it, was rather an odd ball, he thought.

She indeed is a queer one, said Tabby more to himself.

Having said that, he jumped over the window sill and began to snoop around. Chibby wished he'd get off the window before Awra saw the intruder and hurled abuses at him.

157

Get off, will you? she pleaded.

Not until I find those beakers, he replied.

Awra loved playing doctor though she wasn't one. Once a fortnight, Awra would have her children pee into glasses with labels. She would then add a handful of cooked rice into each glass and put them up on the bathroom window and wait. When the time was ripe, she would drain the fluid and examine the colour of the rice. Any sample that crossed the canary-yellow standard was in for an herbal cure. He or she was kept off meat and fish for the rest of the week and was made to swallow bitter herbal concoctions.

To neutralize the colour and counter biliousness, she claimed.

Such of them had an overdose of the bland bottle gourd cooked without seasoning and salt. By and by, the little brigade said,

We'll not pee.

With that, the experiment was suspended, as Awra stood no chance against the determined youth brigade.

I do remember her odious display of the ball of tape worms. How on earth did she manage to flush it out of the fine-fettled one? It sure gave her a great kick to say the least, announced Tabby.

Why don't you come over and have some milk from my bowl? invited Chibby.

I'd love to. But tell me why does milk in your house taste like water? asked Tabby.

It was Awra's habit to dilute milk at the ratio of 1:1 and bring it to boil several times over, never forgetting to keep stirring to keep cream from floating. Likewise, when the curry was brought to boil, she would scoop the gravy with a coconut shell *dovlo,* and drop it, scoop it and drop it many times over into the earthen pot in a slender and cascading stream.

Quite in the manner of a tea-vendor blending the bubbly hot tea at Palghat railway station, thought Babutti who couldn't take his eyes off her dextrous feat.

I'm making sure it has the right consistency, she told her daughter-mother who watched the gravy coursing down like a sulphuric waterfall.

Awra was blind to the follies of her daughter-mother. Christine, a downtown parishioner had a grouse against her. She requested Awra to stop her from harassing her cherubic little one at school.

My Glow Worm can never bring herself to hurt a fly, least of all your daughter. "Pinching her on her cheeks if you please", she murmured.

Awra dismissed her without a second thought. Christine was laid to rest half a century later. That is when Awra brought up the incident to discover that her Glow Worm had indeed harassed the girl by pinching her, as she was temptingly adorable. It was late in the day to make amends except tender an apology to the girl who now lived in Calgary, on the other side of the globe.

In like manner, the boy with the fine fettle, made sure no such complaints about him reached Awra. On one occasion, Mr. Kanute sent word through Martin, the boy's neighbour, to let Awra know that her son was bothersome in school. Eager to comply, Martin walked in the direction of Awra's house, to realize that his naughty peer had a pair of dogs waiting in readiness to give the tittle tattler a chase for his effort. The matter was never pursued. But Awra's mind was in a muddle whenever she heard Babutti sing,

Your winsome boy,
Has lips so sooty
Does anyone know why?
The answer is knotty.

Yonder behind the tree
Twirly blue rings so pretty
Rising to nowhere on a spree
From one so gritty.

Tra la la la la la, tra la la la la la la …

Awra didn't like obscure hints and she shot the messenger with the sweep of a broom. And now it was Babutti's turn. Like Bob, he shot off a letter, but to himself wishing to unravel how the postman was so accurate in delivering the mail to the right person. He wrote,

My dear Babutti,

How are you? I'm out of sorts. When you next visit church, can you ask God to provide snacks during my mid-morning break? I'm forever hungry. One more thing, tables are bothersome. Ask Him to turn eight times eight to whatever number occurs to me at the time I'm being quizzed and please, please make Mr. Kanute's red ink run out. My father hates those red markings in my report card as much as I do. Give my teacher the insight to have more games on the time table. How I love outdoor activities. I promise to be good if these favours are granted. Amen.

Babutti

P.S. I would like to know if you dislike Miss. Seline as much as I do. Treat the matter as confidential.

The letter from Babutti to Babutti gave rise to a hullaballoo in the house. The result, Babutti ended up with more reading, more homework and in his own words, less food. If only he had realized that any mail coming home would be intercepted, he could have averted the painful humiliation that followed.

It was the same Babutti, still a boy, who had once gone missing for a couple of hours. The family went in several directions looking for him. They ran around the avenue, calling out his name. The neighbours too joined in the search. The devout invoked the name of God and one among them said that she would light a candle in thanksgiving at the shrine of St. Lawrence of Karkala, if Babutti was found unharmed. Anxious, the entire party returned home empty handed. Sheer despair made the family take a tour of the rooms all over again and look in every cubby hole.

Call it a mother's third eye, Awra noticed that the box of *boondhi laddoos* that she had placed on the table had gone missing, said Chibby,

Awra gave directions to her other children to follow the scent and sniff out the missing one. She was spot-on. He was right there, sitting in the meat safe gobbling the sugary yellow cakes, without a care in the world. The entire family pummelled him for depriving them of their share. In bad times, they called him *'laddoo'*.

He surely is a chip of the old block, loves food more than life, said Tabby.

Oh, yes! Say that again. I remember what Bishop Bosco who visited Awra to watch the Prudential World Cup on TV, not having a set of his own said, laughed Chibby.

Of course, Tabby remembered the anecdote of a young priest, a bishop in waiting, serving as a chaplain in a convent in the neighbourhood, being narrated ever so often by Awra's folks to tease Babutti.

Babutti and his two friends were the happy altar boys, at daily mass, not so much for the love of the Lord as much as the love of the breakfast served by the nuns after the service, a humble fare though: a cup of steaming coffee and a slice of bread each. Bread in place of rice *kanji* at home was a novelty to the boys. But only till, till the day Babutti realized that the future Bishop at the further end of the room was being served crisp toast with butter, marmalade, a boiled egg and a bowl full of ripe bananas and oranges. Babutti refused to touch the drab stuff on his plate. The nun failed to placate him and that is when the Bishop noticed that all was not hunky-dory with the boys. Being the man that he was, true to his calling, he had the nun lay the table for two.

Not fair, not fair, how could he leave the other two out? Tabby cried out with a grimace.

Ask and you will be given, fight not and you will not be served, haven't you heard that before? rattled off Chibby with her own version from the scriptures she had often heard Awra's community spouting forth.

They who didn't resist, suffered the meagre fare for the rest of their boyhood. All the same, it didn't go easy on Babutti as he had to take all the bullying from his comrades at the altar of God.

Likewise, decades later, the youngest of Awra's children, a girl, walked out of her school in a huff and a puff. She hailed an auto rickshaw to get home which was diametrically opposite the school. Her reason, the aroma of *biriyani* tingled her nose and she suspected that it must be from home and if she didn't get home in time, her mother would have the lion's share of it. An hour later, her father arrived home to discover the driver waiting outside the gate to collect his fare and there was no sign of any *biriyani* as imagined. Well, what followed was amusement. It was apparent that Awra had grown up in the interval of twenty years between Babutti and the last of his siblings.

One could never tell, but surely her children were growing up. When a neighbour's dog broke the neck of their newly hatched chick they mourned like adults. They had a solemn funeral service for the dear departed with no ceremony compromised on. Babutti put on his sister's communion dress, white and frilly, which served as an alb. A coconut frond turned to a tall crucifix, bananas sliced in rings became their host, and a shoe box winged with white trappings from a discarded veil transformed itself to a fitting coffin for the fledgling. A service in Latin, with *Kyrie eleison* and *Mea culpa* were belted out by a choir that could easily put the heavenly cherubim to shame. End of service, the procession of the faithful, escorting the pall-bearers, went around the house to stop beside the trail of morning glory. With a generous sprinkling of water and the final blessing by Babutti and copious tears from the rest, the coffin was lowered into the grave.

Strangely, not one among them grew up to wear the long dress, Chibby said as an afterthought.

Didn't you say that two of those lasses were thorn birds drawn towards the prayerful? enquired Tabby.

You don't understand. It's not the same thing, replied she and turned the other way, a little embarrassed, not wanting to admit that a mother's sage-ness and Awra were worlds apart.

In fact, Tabby understood. He was being tactful for Chibby's sake. Chibby couldn't ever forgive Awra's ineptitude to restrain them from keeping company with those in orders. They were akin to the birds born to impale themselves, Tabby avowed. Visiting Olive Retreat on clandestine dates with the anointed and playing nocturnal coquettes to otherwise prayerful men could easily put Teru's Magdella in the dark, Chibby couldn't help concluding. Thoughtfully filing her claws against the coconut tree, she tried to distract Tabby stating,

Some things are best swept under the carpet in the hope that they die with age.

Do they? Tabby wished to ask, but chose not to speak.

IV

Curiouser and Curiouser

In a while, Tabby interjected once again,

Curiosity killed the cat, so they say. But did Awra care?

He recalled the night when Awra was told of Teru's demise after dinner. Hardly was the news broken, she fired a volley of questions.

How did she die? She wasn't ill, was she? Was she alert to the very end and what were her last words? Did it happen in the hospital with the doctor in attendance, and were you there when death snatched her?

When one of the household said,

Mother, please, did she pull herself together?

But she never rested until she had every detail under her thumb.

I guess she wanted to put some life into her rendering of Teru's death that she was inclined to narrate to anyone who came her way, till another more interesting event took its place, said Chibby.

Awra's mind was forever on an overdrive mode for first-hand information. It happened sooner than expected. Awra's personal maid, Mahankali's alcoholic husband did himself in, in Awra's outhouse using her sash from her clothes line for a noose. When the news was broken to Awra, she asked,

Kalia, when you found him hanging, were his eyes open, was there any trace of life left in him, life enough to tell you how sorry he was? Did he have something to tell you after all?

Mahankali whose name was more than a mouthful and therefore reduced to Kalia by Awra, quite like the British who reduced Benda Kaalu Ooru to Bangalore or Kolikata to Calcutta, Kalia looked incredulously at everyone about and chose to leave her questions unanswered.

Chibby and Tabby too had a taste of Awra's outrageous curiosity which often took a leap in the dark. Standing tall on their hind feet, they were fiercely scratching away at the fibrous trunk of a coconut tree when they almost got crushed under the weight of Awra who dropped on them from the sky, like space debris.

As it happened, the coconut plucker having harvested in abundance, was putting away the fruits in a dark room in the basement. Awra stood on the edge of the topmost step of her house in the backyard, seven in all, and peered. Having sighted neither the coconuts nor the plucker, she held on to the topmost rung of the ladder leaning on the wall and bent further to capture the scene. A split second later, Awra found her curiosity sweeping her off her feet.

The momentum resembled a pole vault and by every Olympian standard Awra qualified. Years later, she was heard recounting how she had to make a split-second decision. She had manoeuvred the incline of the ladder to vault over the cement ledge to enable her to land at the foot of the coconut tree cushioned with weeds. Thanks to the mango showers leading to a prolific germination of seedlings from the womb of the earth. The fall and rise of a super-senior without as much as a mumble or a scratch spoke for her wellness of mind and body, leaving Vincent the handyman, Ananda the coconut plucker and a grandson with wide open mouths. Chibby and Tabby were the only two who yowled fiercely like scolded cats and fled the scene for the love of their lives.

Given her acute inquisitiveness, Awra was expected to show keenness of mind and discernment, but strangely, she suffered from notional idiosyncrasies. Consider the application she forwarded to the District Forest Officer for leave, stating that she would have a headache the following day and hence wouldn't be able to attend duty. Her children will tell you that all she wanted to do was play midwife to her mother-goat in full term who was in labour and help the kids to suckle. Likewise, not even Chibby could digest Awra's assumption that someone with a sprawling hip had either an active life or she had a false bottom. If her housemaid was not her usual chirpy self, she inferred that she was starved of warmth from her man. Her knowledge of electronics was equally appalling. When a friend called and the network being poor, in a matter of fact way she said,

Modi must be making too many calls tracking black money and the network is sure to be mobbed by reviews on de-and-re-monetization.

It's mind boggling. She is getting curiouser and curiouser by the day, thought the two and gave up as electronics and economics was not their forte.

But Tabby couldn't absolve Awra of not having stood by Celia who was repeatedly raped by her father-in-law, with her husband and mother-in-law looking the other way. Awra's defense,

How could she speak up? It is inadmissible for a daughter-in-law to jeopardize the reputation of her household.

Often Chibby was at a loss for words to describe Awra's servitude. She fetched change of clothes for her husband and fixed his bath water and went down on her knees to help him get into his pair of polished sandals or shoes. She parted his hair after having creamed it, to set it for the day. Chibby was equally stupefied to see her serve him his meals and clean up after him. Her justification,

He is a man.

V

Logging Memories

Why does Awra look so lost whenever she opens the black box which belonged to her husband? Tabby asked.

Oh, that one. It is full of memorabilia, Chibby replied wondering what Tabby had to do with it.

Tabby had often seen her pull out a pair of glasses which belonged to her long dead husband and look through them, for something beyond recall. Did she expect to see what her husband had perceived? In any case, one of the lenses had a mangled hole in it as if a meteor had shot through it. Tabby wondered if the old man's life had escaped through his eye leaving behind a star-hole. Sometimes, she pulled out a tiny silver box. Each time she opened it, she couldn't help sniffing it, and invariably ended up sneezing a million times, 'achoo'. It was his monogramed snuff box with the engraved letters – PD on it, Chibby informed her curious companion.

Quite like the virtual times when Awra and her children went into vicarious sneezing bouts, their nostrils tingled by the pungent snuff that was flying around after the sniffing session by PD. Awra couldn't help visualising the old man who was adept at tapping an accurate amount of the silky brown tobacco precipitate from that silver receptacle into the middle of his left palm with ritualistic deliberation, tap, tap, tap. Having done, he would click shut the box and go on to pulverise the dust with his right thumb, with the other four fingers serving as base to the palm to accelerate the action, with the dedication of an alchemist at work. He'd then pick a chock-full of the fiery stuff between his thumb and forefinger and brush the rest with a clap clap of both the palms sliding off over the other as if he were keeping an intoxicated qawwali beat to a song. Those in his proximity were caught in the dust up, some sneezing instantly while others were under duress to suspend their thoughts and actions to let the sneezes work their way out through the tingling tunnels, at their own pace. No one was spared to utter the 'Bless You' to check their souls from escaping with the achoos. The finale came with PD walking around with his hands locked behind his back with the dust held in a tight pinch, unperturbed by the goings on, and a look of expectant consummation on his countenance. At the ominous moment when all seemed to have settled down, he deposited the stuff into his accommodating nostrils with deliberated shoves and pushes. The act accomplished, they reciprocated with a resounding acknowledgement. Taking a cue, PD's two boys ran helter skelter looking for his snuff towel to help him muffle the announcement and clean up the act.

Pacifying her tingling nose with a gentle knead, Awra ran her fingers over the West End watch that belonged to PD, seemingly to cajole it to tick again. When no such thing happened, she gave it a joggle to churn its insides. The hands stood still refusing to budge, yet she wore it on her wrist and let it stay there for the rest of her exploration. Then out came a tiny bundle wrapped in her husband's discarded *lungi*. It was an opaque looking ribbed goblet with myriad scratches and one or two chipped gashes at the rim-end. She ran her fingers over it and held it by the stem and appeared pensive. Tabby didn't quite comprehend what the brouhaha was all about that she had treasured it as if it were a prized *lladro*.

How was Tabby to know that Awra was running over the roll call of inexhaustible number of men who had lipped the cup? How was anyone to know that those were the times when prohibition was clamped, yet a time when families surreptitiously brewed their own liquor in their backyards to be served at a feast or a wedding? They kept the liquid buried under the coconut trees in ceramic jars. No dog or cop could sniff it out. Such was the care taken to keep off talebearers to guard tradition. The fiery liquid was brought out on occasions and the host filled the goblet to the brim. It then moved from one eager hand to another. Each took a generous sip and swilling it in his mouth gulped it down. Sealing the act with a smack of lips and a raucous clearing of throat or with a stiff quiver of the shoulders, they complimented the quality of the brew and the generosity of the host.

Awra saw Domingo, a neighbour to the Dominicans, deftly twirl his bushy moustache and run his tongue over his lips hidden under it to lick any trace of the spirit. He had waited for his turn to have one more swig of the igneous stuff, when the host refilled the goblet for a second and hoping that he would replenish it for a third round as well. She remembered having seen Juan *Bappu* turn gregarious as the tingling liquid trickled down his gut and knocked his knees weak. On the contrary, Savehr *Maam* wore an idiotic look with a permanent grin on his face. Awra couldn't tell why Pokkaam reclined his head over Feddy *Aab's* shoulder and wept copiously. Each time they met, the cup was filled to the brim with the pungent brew extracted out of the reeking cashew fruit, he broke down. Nostalgic, Awra opened her eyes and peered into the cup and lifted it bottoms up waiting for the tipple to flow on to her tongue. Nothing happened as the cup was dry. She snapped out of her reverie and put away the *idru.*

Following this, Awra was seen pulling out a royal blue velvet purse from which emerged a wedding band, the one she had given PD those many years ago, as a sign of her undying commitment. She toyed with it for a while and pushed it onto her gnarled little finger on the left hand. Neither Chibby nor Tabby could read the tumultuous thoughts coursing through her mind and the emotions dancing on her countenance. Of course, she looked ludicrous with those glasses, the wedding band, the wrist watch and a grey monkey cap. At intervals, she singled out the silver *kanakadi* from his key bunch to dig her ears with an orgasmic sense of pleasure and examine the brown wax with gratification. When she could excavate no more, she used the intricate toothpick, moving slackly on a ring among the bunch of complex tools, to loosen tartar from the remnant of a pair of her grey teeth. Simultaneously, a magnifying glass danced over the bleached pages of what looked like a diary of sorts. Now she skimmed and now she scanned some of the entries. Certain jottings, she read out loud, some others she mulled over with eyes shut tight and some she re-read running her finger over every line.

December 26, 1945: What on earth was that prayer about? A long enough life to welcome our great grandchildren, when I hadn't yet begun on children? I couldn't quite say Amen as I was in a hurry to consummate my marriage. She is a handful.

November 17, 1970: Mr. 'D' What have you done? How did she land in your well? I served as your alibi before men, but who will save you before God? Come clean Mr. D., come clean.

August 20, 1980: Whoever thought that the red-capped one would lust after money? How could he bring himself to sleep on it literally?

May 23, 1996: It's not ethical. To deny him his birth right. I must will it to whom it's due.

June 10, 2002: In the end, nothing matters, but how you have lived! May God give her the grace to mend her ways.

June 11, 2002: It took me long to discern. Only one of them may be relied upon and no other.

Such cryptic entries baffled Awra. She couldn't digest the fact that he had logged away private thoughts to which she was not privy. Shutting the book abruptly she walked away in a huff only to return to open another box, her own. But it was way too small, yet holding an unusual assortment of queer merchandise: reams of coloured streamers faded in patches: red, blue, pink, yellow and green. When Chibby tried her hand at unrolling them in a playful mood, Awra denied her the pleasure reproving her friskiness with,

No, Chiboh, no! These are my wedding decorations.

Awra then spotted a small bottle of *Chanel*, which had no character having lost its colour and scent from aging; two large sachets of soap nuts; several cakes of soap- Dr. White for the white linen and the blue *Kasturi* bars to wash the coloured clothes with; the scented Pears to wash her face with, the *Hamam* for the rest of her body; besides, there was a labelled brown paper bag with band aid, gauze and a couple of unused blades and a pair of scissors; a purse with as many compartments as there were envelopes with bills of varying denominations, counted and the amount marked on the envelope; a pile of birthday cards she had received over the years; a bundle of her daughter's love letters which she had deftly hidden from her as she didn't want a daughter of hers marrying the descendant of a butler; portraits of herself as a young girl and the dried up umbilical cords of some of her children. She also brought out a heavy and crude scale suspended by link chains, made of steel.

175

Was that the scale she stole from her daughter? **Tabby** wished to ask someone to verify.

Awra was incapable of trusting anyone. She harboured suspicions against everyone, including the milkman and the storekeeper from where she got her monthly provisions. She therefore thought it useful to keep the scale hidden from her daughter so that she could weigh her supply ranging from onions to tomatoes, sugar to salt, gram for gram, and sometimes compare one store with another. There was also a tiny figurine of a pig among keepsakes in the box.

A pig, did you say? What did she have to do with a pig? asked Tabby with whiskers raised.

Well, yes. A pig, you heard me right, said Chibby.

The figurine reminded her of Prince whom she had raised for two years.

Was that the one she was ragged about no end by her husband to the amusement of her children?

Yes, the very same.

Her husband didn't let Awra forget about how she massaged Prince' neck who lay supine at her feminine touch. For as long as her reassuring hand was on his neck, he didn't mind the gag in his mouth and the fetters on his limbs. He was prepared to lie still and ignore the shackles. He didn't expect

Dukor Charlie to sink the knife deep into his throat to slash the jugular vein. He died a slow death as he watched his life force gushing out of him into a deep utensil. Charlie kept whipping it to keep it creamy. The idea was to prevent it from coagulating until it was heated on slow fire turning it into a crumbly mix, to be thrown into every indigenous preparation for authentic flavour. While for Prince, the bloody picture made everything appear hazy. Like will-o'-the- wisp, Awra was there by his side one moment and she wasn't there the next when he wanted to ask her what was happening to him. Her husband claimed that Prince Gooty had an expression of utter dismay in his eyes when he gave up his breath, that he was unlikely to get over the deception, when he discovered he was dead.

Chibby, you take care. Hobnobbing with the likes of her is not without dangers. Never know what's playing on her mind. Not everyone is a Teru. Mankind is indeed capricious.

VI

Darkness to Light

So, forewarning his companion, Tabby walked home to the comfort of his seat by the fireside. That's where he found a sapless silhouette of Teru intently scanning a whirl of negatives against the luminous flame from a kerosene lamp, something someone had pulled out of a camera and left unattended. She ignored Tabby as if he didn't matter anymore.

Tabby couldn't make sense of her interest in something as lacklustre as blotches of dark and light. This frame was one of a row of half-naked people with receding hairline and dangling ponytails at the nape of their necks and a cord running across their chest diagonally, from shoulder to hip. They were seated cross legged on the floor in a straight line with their right hands resting on banana leaves spread before them, expectantly waiting for a meal to be served. Bent over them was one of their kind with a bucket in one hand and a tilted ladle in the other, with no trace of food anywhere. A meal with no food? Tabby was clueless as to the intent of the image.

Teru next gawked at the frame of a wrinkled old man with a caved abdomen and thin arms wired up with purple veins. A yoke placed on his shoulders, he was captured doing the rounds painstakingly at an oil press. Tabby recognized this one. He had been at it for a life time and he would be at it till he had outlived his karma of having shed blood at a Hindu-Muslim riot during a communal insurrection.

The ensuing one, was a replica of a coffin. Looking over Teru's shoulder, Tabby saw the likeness of Awra sitting in a coffin and putting out her hand in the manner of a destitute seeking alms. He dismissed it as a mere figment of his imagination as he had seen Awra just a while ago looking fit as a fiddle. In fact, he had heard her nit- picking about the way the house was being run by her son and blamed the itchy inflammation on her feet to the aromatic mutton stew she had had for dinner. Tabby regretted not having brought Chibby along. She with her feminine intuition was sure to know what these films were about. Before he could count on a period to stop these erratic pictures and thoughts coursing through his mind, he saw the curly-whirly film drop to the ground and Teru breeze past him into nowhere. He stood still, no longer able to fathom the direction she took. Disappointed, Tabby comforted himself with the thought that it was now up to her to work her way out from darkness to light. But if he were to rationalise the occurrence, he might have thought,

It was an inane encounter, perhaps a necessary one, transporting her from one way of life to another.

VII

The Twilight Hour

At almost ninety-four, Awra's transition from one state of being to another was imminent. But there was no predicting, when and how. Would she depart without a warning like Teru did or would she customize her exit with the regimented fanfare she was so accustomed to? At the chosen hour and time as always: wake up at five a.m. to attend to nature's call, return to bed at quarter past five, rise at half past six, have tea at a quarter to seven and a colossal bowl of oats half an hour hence, breakfast at a quarter past that hour along with a banana or two to push it down her throat, tea again at nine a.m., a bowl of fruit at half past ten, a glass of buttermilk at eleven, lunch at one p.m., tea with light snacks at four, a ritual bath at her whim, but between tea and dinner, dinner at eight p.m. and retire to bed by nine p.m., and the breathless schedule could be interrupted only to draw her last breath at ..., no one could tell, not even Awra, much to her chagrin. Or would she linger on till every cell of her being died one by one, atoning for breaking the tenets of Moses. Chibby was sure to have a point of view, he thought. When he next called on Chibby, in a matter-of-fact tone she said,

Take it from me that she has everything in place.

You mean that she'll have an orchestrated exit?

As you live, so you die. She has lived life on her own terms and she is sure to take leave in a like manner.

Now this is beyond me. Would death come riding on a chariot to escort her? asked Tabby and looked at his companion expectantly.

To learn that Awra had been preparing for the curtain call, a little at a time, had him bring his right paw to his chin and stare in anticipation of an explanation to follow.

I've seen her display all her jewellery on the table, put them on piece by piece and take them off repeatedly only to throw them into a pile, only to re-allot them afresh, and sit before them in yogic contemplation, eyes shut. But her skittish mind always has trouble in assigning specific lots to her daughters who would be heir to them. When she does part with them, she is likely to do so with expectations, Chibby reminisced.

What does she want? asked Tabby.

The usual, their time, the one thing they are most reluctant to give.

I've witnessed the way she apportioned her belongings to those who are entitled to them. Not a spoon or a ladle got left out except Babutti. He had no place in her scheme of things. With great pleasure, she unfurled and read the scroll *ad nauseam*. Her will, was a mile long, with sheets and sheets of foolscap paper stapled together into a ream, Chibby spoke with ardour.

On her planned exit, she had written therein,

No hospitalization, no Ryle's tube, no surgery. Wish to breeze through the last lap like a champ.

She seems to know what she wants, doesn't she, intoned Tabby.

As an afterthought, she has left instructions to Babutti, in fact, a codicil, said Chibby and began to read out,

'Serve tea and Marie biscuits to all who attend my graveside service, provide breakfast to those who make it to the prayer service at the Weeks Mind and dinner to members of the family at the Memorial

Service. Bills to be paid from the khaki envelope set aside in the blue pouch.'

Awra wanted none of her offspring to take credit for any of the service provided on her behalf. She believed in a dignified exit having no obligation to anyone, stated Chibby.

She leaves nothing to chance, does she? said Tabby in admiration.

He admired her for thinking like a man, but didn't say so as he didn't wish to appear gender biased and get into a tiff with Chibby.

Besides, I've overheard her nail down her confessor, to tell her if God is a fact or an opinion, resumed Chibby with great enthusiasm.

For someone who rolls the beads all the time, that's surprising! But why? Tabby enquired.

So, she could live the rest of her life in reparation or indulgence to make up for the lean times she had endured. And schedule the inevitable exit, I guess. She is like Thomas, replied Chibby.

Remember how Teru left, without as much as a goodbye, with no flourish, no resistance and a calmness that was so unlike her. God must be a choice mankind makes, replied Tabby as an afterthought, to the envy of a sceptic like Awra and made haste to leave, being an agnostic himself.

Awra had some more questions lined up for the Confessor, and among them was the one that rankled her the most. She had spent an entire morning psyching herself to ask him if he believed in heaven and hell.

You are likely to tell me that such issues don't matter to us. But, what do you think requires more wisdom, giving the right answers or posing the right questions? Is it because of her questions that her confessor no longer visits her or is it because he didn't have the answer? Tabby asked and Chibby was not disposed to respond.

Tabby was aware of a R.I.P. holder that Awra had kept in readiness to be taken to the undertaker to prepare her for her final journey when death knocked on her door. She had packed a rich blue brocade sari and a white *hakoba* blouse to go with it; a rosary given to her by daughter-mother with roses carved on the wooden beads; an old crucifix measuring the length of her palm, which had been thrust into the hands of her parents-in-law, and those before and after them, when their remains were laid out for final viewing; Mary's medal looped onto a red ribbon conferred by Christian Mother's Society to adorn her neck; and a lace-edged scarf to have her face covered before the coffin was nailed closed. Occasionally, the paraphernalia would be aired out in the sun to have them smelling fresh, unlike death, she claimed. And it had a second envelope, sealed and addressed to the undertaker, to be broken open when she was gone.

What is in it? Tabby asked losing no time.

Chibby in explanation said,

Her epitaph:

Here rests B-A-I- BAI.
She lived, fullest.
26.9.1923 –

Tabby who detested those shallow overstated outbursts on headstones appreciated Awra's earthy simplicity of thought and said,

An epitaph that doesn't sound like one.

An epitaph it is, said Chibby in a sombre mood and crossed herself to put off the thought of the dusky hour.

Chapter 6

LOVE OF LIFE

I

Joie de Vivre

Awra lives on.

Chibby didn't savour the thought of a life without Awra around. And it set Tabby thinking about Teru.

Would Awra resist death or would she give herself up as she did to her husband's every whim and fancy? Would she revisit life as Teru did? contemplated Tabby.

If you had the sage-ness you wouldn't ask so many questions just because Awra revelled in asking the type of questions she ought not to have asked in the first place, snapped Chibby.

For a change, Tabby was astonished to hear Chibby's objective admission of Awra's limitations. Besides, she was all ears when Tabby began to showcase the landmarks Awra was likely to haunt from the other side of the bank.

Tabby vouched for it that she was sure to come home first thing at dawn. To lay her hands on the local newspaper before anyone else did. To visit page twelve replete with obituaries of the dead. There she would find pictures of kindred souls of her generation whom she would frenetically place by name, age, place and occupation. With the younger ones, she would cross their age and names with those of her children or grandchildren to establish contemporaneity. If someone went before time, she would make it her business to infer and sometimes establish the cause of demise and come to believe in it by the end of the day. As was her habit, she seldom refrained from drawing up the family tree. Based on their surname and the status of the deceased, she deduced who would be at the funeral and how plain or ceremonious the occasion was likely to be. If the page featured anyone from her parish, she'd be restless till she got the sacristan online to check out the antecedents of the one numbered among the dead.

Awra would then flip the other pages as she was disposed to lap up reports of the elderly whose necks were slit for gain. She would follow up on the stories and move abreast with the investigating cops to nab the suspects. Her interest in accounts of devastation by earthquakes, storms and torrential rain was equally enthusiastic. But her itch for the vagaries of weather was selective, limited to places where her own lived.

Awra was unlikely to miss the matrimonial advertisement which appeared weekly in the papers, especially those of her own community. Such advertisements gave her enough ammunition and entertainment to keep her engaged through the day.

How tall is tall? How fair is fair? she would ask amused.

She would be suspicious of appendages like,

'A divorcé may apply' or 'A slight deformity could be overlooked.'

The only exception was of an advertisement which moved her to tears when a boy of five appeared on the matrimonial column seeking a spouse for his widowed mother,

'Looking for a father. Anyone who has it in him, a heart and a willingness, to cheer my mother may apply.'

Frantically, Awra applied her ingenuity to make herself useful, but often not knowing who it was she was set out to help proved to be her undoing. Given the age, qualifications of the eligible grooms and comely brides and their employment status, she would instantly begin making matches for the applicant. She would summon her daughter-in-law and tell her of a certain groom who was placed in the US of America, who could make an ideal match for her niece from Singapore, a lass just about graduating from school. If you told her that it wasn't viable as the girl was way too young and still schooling, she would get emotional followed by an outburst,

What a shame, what a shame. I like your sister's genial ways and I expect her daughter to have taken after her, and therefore I thought that, ...

Her discourse was interrupted by a counter response,

Who is the bloke anyway?

Abashed, Awra would reply,

I'll figure that out by and by. But don't you think, ... And you need not disclose the father's antecedents, I mean the circumstances of his parentage, and so she would go on and on.

At another time, just because the matrimonial advertiser happened to belong to the clan of the Farias', she would get hold of visiting kinsfolk to quiz them about the clique who once lived in Kadri when she was a girl, a certain Inthru Farias, a Jacqua Farias, a Santhan Farias, an Ijju Farias, all Farias'. She would then think of girls in her circle of family and friends to match them with their supposed progeny whose existence and status she had no clue to, not having kept up with the Joneses throughout life.

It is a most annoying preoccupation that she has taken to of late, to say the least, complained Chibby.

During these years, many a match was made and unmade relentlessly. Tabby wasn't sure if Awra would be able to break free from the die-hard preoccupation to see young people coupled, particularly those in her social circle.

She is an all-out romantic for sure, teased Tabby.

That she is, besides being engaged with a thousand other interests, cut in Chibby.

Come rain or shine, Awra was unlikely to give the fish market at Urwa a miss, thought Tabby with his mouth salivating.

When the clock strikes ten, like an addict snorting dope she'd inhale the scent of fresh fish, and she is certain to go after it to the market place, wagered Tabby.

Given its vantage point, Awra is apt to sit atop the cash counter in stall No.6. and keep an eye on Saroja who was notorious for what her nimble fingers could do. The rest of the fisher folk depended on her surgical skills to replace the discoloured gills, of fish from yesterday, with layers of ruddy ones she would sparingly extract from the catch of the day. And with the dexterity of Dr. Christiaan Barnard, transplant them, without a heart. She seldom dyed it *kumkum* red as she lived in fear of being caught red-handed as it happened once, Tabby continued.

Awra, as accustomed to, would open the gill of a humongous pomfret and come close to feeling the goop when an uncharacteristic sappy fluid would run past her fingers brushing the face of the gilled one with a blush. And with it would come off the transplant and the rotting whiff. Irked, Awra was likely to hold up the detached gill and call her a *donghi, a dokebaaz,* loud enough for everyone to hear, as she had once done in the past. The showdown would have the lady docked and customers were likely to drift elsewhere to look for their ware. That apart, Awra wouldn't be able to resist running her fingers over the sleek ladyfish to gauge as to how many servings she could get out of her or tap one cockle atop another and crack them inside out to ascertain if they were fleshy, thought Tabby. No matter how adept Awra had become at bargaining with the fisherwomen, at this far from regulated market, the fisher folk always had the last word. Sitting where she was, Awra would relish every haggling encounter and smack her lips if a customer got an edge over the fishmonger.

They all began by accosting the customers with the generic courtesy,

Porbule, Akka, Bayamma, inchi ora bale, thule encha undu, thaja halwa da lekka. Jeeva da meen. Bale Anna.

And if the fisherwoman saw a vermilion dot on a male customer's forehead she would endearingly call out,

Bale enna Krishna, playing the coquette to win him over.

Babutti who is now a man in his own right is known to take on the gabby women and tease them tooth for tooth. Being aware of the tricks of the trade, if the fisherwoman quoted Rs. 1,200/- for a giant-sized king-fish, he would instantly slash the figure by fifty percent. He would regale her with tales of how his wife had given him a sound thrashing for having taken home an overpriced butter fish the last time. So much so, he had to consider seeing an orthopaedic to check out his bundle of rattling bones, he claimed. The story tickled her no end, but it surely wasn't enough to get her to relent. The two would continue to haggle, with him raising and her lowering the bar a little at a time till the deal was clinched, and him rewarding her with *baksheesh* for goodwill. And there were those who eyed the fish but were not willing to pay. To make it worse, they had no humour to put some fun into the haggling to hammer out a deal. Such earned not only a tongue lashing but also a dousing from head to toe with a tub full of fishy water. The unfortunate victim wouldn't dare venture into the place for a long time to come.

Awra was not likely to give any of it a miss, said Chibby.

Returning home, Awra would grudgingly watch the maid who would have replaced her even before she had turned cold, albeit for the skill with which she cut the fish seated on Awra's customized cutting stool. The maid had the expertise of a nimble-fingered surgeon. Her deft hands, seizing the slithery fish at both ends, moved from left to right and right to left. Running it ever so lightly and briskly over the *adolo* to de-scale the fish.

Awra was certain to be tempted to stroke her seven cats playing Dog and the Bone seated around the tray of fish. They sat waiting for an unguarded moment to snatch the fish and scoot from the place. Awra often spoke regretfully of the day when she had wielded a knife at one of the cats for stealing a mackerel from right under her nose, which left the cat with a gaping hole in the head and a gory scene behind. And all fled including Chibby. Thereafter, whenever Awra cut fish, like Birbal's proverbial twice bitten cat, they remained seated at a safe distance with trepidation and desire warring with each other.

Count yourself lucky Chibbo that you are in one piece. Why don't you and our kittens move in with me? asked Tabby apprehensively.

Tabby was almost seething when he learnt about how five of Chibby's companions were trapped by Awra's husband and disposed of close to the International Airport at Kenjaar.

They were released, unlike the Mendons who pushed the new-borns into a bag and dropped it into a bucket full of water, and when the kittens writhed no more flung it into the culvert over the wall, so, Chibby tried to console her mate.

Awra unaware of their shipment, didn't give up her search for her feline diversions. She looked at the hooting barn owl in the church yard with suspicion and wondered whether he had a hand in their disappearance. She had been told that owls could make a meal of eyes, especially those from cats. The blind cats would then fall into a ditch and starve themselves to death or be pecked eaten by the crows, unable to put up a fight or make a comeback home. All the same, Tabby had a hunch that Awra would seek them out in death and be their consolation. Just as she would be on the lookout for Prince Gooty, who expected her to offer more than an apology for furtively robbing him of life.

It was highly unlikely that Prince would ever trust his neck to her. It would be foolish to befriend her a second time at the risk of having his throat slit at the hands of a lady whom he loved more than he did his sow, gabbled Tabby.

Awra who made much of her childhood was sure to return to her carefree days from the netherworld. Tabby was convinced that she'd revisit her zest-filled yesterdays to facilitate her transition from one state of being to the other. He corroborated it with a peek into Awra's dossier and happily said,

She will no longer walk, but hop skip and jump along the after-death-trail to return to the familiar terrain.

Awra was sure to walk the mile from home to her *Bappu's* office at Kodialbail, despite all the commotion, traffic and the people who had replaced a serene way of life she had known in her childhood. A life she so cherished. She had lived amid the sprawling wilderness which flanked the fields and coconut groves. An occasional man leading his cattle to graze somewhere green, a cyclist with heaps of spinach and radish being ferried to the local market, notwithstanding the sight of the scavenger who carried the night soil in a bucket on his head, at times announcing his presence were familiar sights. Awra is sure to fancy them over the razzmatazz of the contemporary Mall culture, which she so resented.

On arrival, she would discover that a bishop, was in the seat at the diocesan house, but not her *Bappu*, there would not be the B-A-I- *Bai salaam* of her formative days, not the camaraderie and the hospitality that had defined her childhood for her.

Disheartened, Awra would turn back, only to slow down at the copper-pod tree in bloom in the bishop's yard. She'd hover about the place waiting for the golden yellow bloom to shower her with a soft reception. She was bound to wear a wreath and wristbands of the blooms she was adept at stringing together. And tread a slow measure with her imaginary knight leading her into an unruffled world, not letting the current debilitating chaos to supersede her happy memories. She would linger on to savour this overpowering experience by chalking out a grid on the ground with eight boxes in rows of two. Standing at one end, she would debate if she should hop zigzag through the squares on her right leg or make a straight run leaping with a leg each in the boxes, one or two rows at a time, and be done with it. She would soon give up the idea as a contest is no contest with no one to challenge her prowess at the game. Awra would move on.

On her way, she wouldn't be able to resist a visit to her alma mater for old times' sake, only to be disillusioned. The classes were too large and for some reason the teacher was bawling all the time. She no longer resembled the Ma'ams of yesteryears with accordion pleated skirts, tucked in blouses and slip-ons that gave one an air of professionalism. Their perfectly coiffed hair and buxom fullness which enabled them to carry their portfolio was missing. The French lessons were replaced by Kanarese and she couldn't make head or tail of it. The English they spoke sounded more like a local dialect. The lady in charge of the classroom was thin as a reed and her lacklustre performance would make Awra flee. School wasn't pleasurable anymore.

The pandemonium along the way reminded her of her 1964 trip to Bombay, accompanied by her husband in honour of the Eucharistic Congress, which left her with a feeling of a lot to be desired.

I neither saw the Pope nor received the Eucharist, she complained, to all and sundry on her return.

She was unlikely to get over her small moments which she so tried to forget, which the rest of the world worked hard to keep alive.

Are you talking about the time when she complained to her tall husband that she couldn't see a thing? enquired Tabby.

Yes, yes, the very same act when her husband told her that if she couldn't see the Pope standing, she must try getting a glimpse of him, sitting down. Trusting him implicitly as always, she did just that. Soon it dawned upon her that it was stupid of her not to have seen through what he was getting at. How could she have taken him literally? She was not going to be invited to sit on his shoulders and get a worldview, was she? But that she didn't have the presence of mind to detect his sarcasm embarrassed her no end, even long after the act, replied a peeved Chibby.

So much for her tacit dependence on her husband, commented Tabby.

Walking down the slope along a choked up road full of smoke belching vehicles, she would make a stop at London *vaddo*, only to discover that her house no longer stood where she had left it standing, on the day she left it to join her husband in marriage. In its place stood an unfamiliar structure walled on all sides and guarded by barking dogs. The only familiar

landmarks were Terry's childhood home next door
with an open portico and the same old neighbourly
mango tree which had generously dropped fruits
on to her side of the house which she picked up,
something a child learnt to exercise by a natural right
to proximity and not any other. No one objected to
what she did, least of all the mango tree.

Awra would be in half a mind to step in at Terry's
and pick up a stone or two and pelt at the clusters of
green mangoes. That is when she would be sure to
notice the long *vakhil baank,* a twin of the one which
had adorned the veranda of her own house of yore.
Soon, a shadow would cut her line of vision, and she'd
see Terry cross from one end of the house to another,
clearing the passage and drawing her attention to the
mantelshelf. It bore the same century old menorah
adorning the crucifix above the altar on the wall.
The altar was crowded with the holy family and a
pantheon of angels and saints. She would be quick to
drop the stones and make the sign of the cross. Her
eyes would turn moist at the thought of not having
been permitted to keep any of the memorabilia that
her parents so treasured at their altar, especially the
tiny Italian statuettes of Mother Mary with the infant,
with a delicately crafted font at her feet for holy water.
Dattu's family laid seize to all the artefacts and there
ended the matter.

Each time she visited her nephew, she was
overpowered by a sense of *deja vu* at the sight of that
mantelshelf in the drawing room which belonged to
her mother.

That's where Mama kept her jewellery. And that jewel box, how I coveted it. Mama wouldn't give it to me, Awra nearly wept, said a gloomy Chibby.

It goes to Dattu's wife, when he gets himself one, Mama announced, Awra often recollected.

Awra couldn't forgive *Dattu* for the way he had Mama wrapped around his little finger. Only to swipe her of her jewellery, piece by piece. He left her bare-necked with not a piece to prettify her delicate frame. Perturbed, she would recline against the wall with eyes shut tightly to obliterate her painful past. When she thinks that she is just about done, a series of fresh images, not necessarily painful, in fact, some of them amusing on hind sight would serenade before her, almost like a Disney Parade in progress.

Among them was the picture of a little girl getting into a shallow stream behind her house every afternoon. To catch the tiny fish with their reckless agility with the intention of bottling and breeding them at home. Invariably, she found them floating in the carafe by about the third day. It is then that she saw the well that the Adhikaris owned, from which her mother drew water, on a regular basis for cooking. The Adhikaris were in for a shock to discover an occasional mercurial tempered creature having a rollicking time in their copper pot where they stored water for cooking. At the first whiff of defilement, they went snooping around to discover not an occasional minnow, but shoals of them having a boisterous time in the well, having dodged the pony-tailed Brahman. Soon after began the purification ritual. Curious, the girl had watched the arrival of a half-clad priest with his band of caste assistants to drain out every drop of water from the well and with it the unsuspecting elfin members.

The little girl standing at a safe distance heard the priest chant mantras and burn incense sticks and direct puffs of smoke into the well with the circular sweep of his hand. She saw him drop petals and red dust and rice into the depth. It was days before the well surged with sweet drinking water, but every couple of months the ritual was repeated with the resurgence of life in the unfathomable deep. A perplexed Adhikari was told by the priest in no uncertain terms that he was being haunted by an ancestor whose annual funeral rite had not been kept up by his father. To placate the unhappy soul, he was ordered to have a *homa* done and feed the destitute and give generously to charity.

Awra's adult and out worldly perspective is sure to make her squirm at this mumbo-jumbo, claimed Chibby with a swagger.

Would Awra chastise herself for her ill-placed perseverance of breeding fish? asked Tabby.

Chibby conceded that a brahman well could never be their habitat, something that Awra didn't know at the time. Nor did she know that the mantras stood no chance before the minnows.

199

Tabby and Chibby laughed themselves hoarse each time they remembered the incident and wondered if a spectral Awra would revisit the episode and give the brahman descendants a run for their rigidity. Of course, the senior Adhikari, had joined his ancestors, but the "well" stood as a mute testimony to a girl who dropped bottles of fish everyday into its inviting womb.

The visit to the Adhikari "well" was sure to rouse Awra's memories. Of the time when Babutti, by now an adult and the father of a daughter, was stricken with a fever that raged on for forty-two days and forty-three nights. No pundit could restore his well- being and it had Awra in a fix. She had paid a clandestine visit to the astrologer, the same one, who had rubbed against her grain. He was discomposed by the hubbub he saw behind his calculations, wrought by the unsettled spirits at 'Bethel', now residence to Babutti.

The reason, a voluminous peepal tree that covered more than half the landscape at 'Bethel' had been felled. It was so voluminous, that it took two elephants to load the trunk on to a truck. With a parched tongue, a lost look and a slight tremor in his fingers, the bedecked astrologer squeaked,

Ram Ram, that old tree was home to countless benign spirits, of birds, of beasts and men too. It was pulsating with life. Look what has been done to them. They are now scattered and rendered homeless. To avenge their displacement, they have entered Babutti's house for shelter.

Now, hurry home. Get a priest, to bless the house and appease the dishevelled spirits, those peaceful dwellers.

If I were you, I'd invite them over to live in the house and become my guardian spirits. Babutti will bounce back by and by. Make peace with the spirits, make peace, pleaded the astrologer and became incommunicado having slipped into a trance.

Awra would surely stop by at 'Bethel', to scan the cubbyholes and corners, the loft and the shelves, the boxes and the niches on the wall where a kerosene lamp or a statue stood to see if she could locate any of them. Being dead, she would be able to spot them, that is, if there was any credence to the priest's mutterings, thought the felines.

But before Awra did that, she'd make sure to visit the Rasquinhas in Terry's neighbourhood, who had over a dozen children, some of whom were her contemporaries. She was sure to ascertain if they in turn had as many children as their forefathers did. As a girl, she often wondered why it was that her mother bore only two children. She had tried asking her mother,

Mama, why can't you make more babies?

Her Mama blushed and had no answers to give, with her father having left the earthly abode by then. When no answers came by, she persisted,

Mama won't Seraphina's husband come back? Why was he driven away Mama? Why doesn't he visit his wife and the new-born baby?

There was no way the mother could explain to Awra that it was not the done thing for a husband to seek personal time with his wife during the postpartum care at her mother's place, so soon after the birth of a baby. It was unheard of for a husband to jump over the compound wall, climb the roof of the house, move a few tiles and slip into her room when the rest of the house was asleep. She couldn't tell her that Seraphina, all of sixteen at the time, was terrified of his advances and his insatiable libido. So soon after the birth trauma, all she could think of was call out to her *Akhai*, loud enough to wake up the dead. *Akhai,* a bead-rolling spinster and virtuous matriarch of the house at that and a light sleeper too, took hold of the broom left under the cradle to ward off the evil forces. She gave him so sound a thrashing that it woke up the rest of the household. And they followed suit. He took off on his heels and was never heard of for the next three years. And she couldn't tell Awra that that was the reason why there was a gap of four years between the two younglings of Seraphina, a quaint one for the times when cradles never stopped rocking till couples had had all their children, anywhere between a dozen to a dozen and a half.

Seraphina had long left for the world of the dead. Awra had lost track of the family and their household had passed through several generations and the Rasquinhas were a forgotten lot. But not Alice who lived yards away from the Rasquinhas, who had given up her ghost a long time ago. She had left behind her shadow on her children for something she did, with and without the endorsement of those around her. Alice being who she was, an efficient and accomplished lady, wasn't brow beaten by poverty. So much so, she was sought after by the landed gentry, particularly a landlord of a well-known *Guthu* to run his household and attend to his highborn but barren wife. By and by, the lady of the house felt a terrible compunction that she would fail her husband, if she left him without a male heir, any heir, to continue his lineage. Who better than Alice to play handmaiden? Which she did. She went on to give birth to four children whose reputation was eclipsed by a tag that refused to leave them. They were labelled 'Hybrids.' The acceptance and status she had earned among the *Guthu* eluded her when it came to her own kind. Awra remembered her neighbours warning her, to keep off the social scum.

Awra was unable to understand the *ménage à trois* at work in the *Guthu* household even after a lapse of seventy years. Modernism had exposed her to the concept of gay marriages. How she wished to find out what such couples did to express themselves but for the fact that she asked the conservatives who dodged her questions. She was equally flummoxed by live in partners and was ever curious to find out what the objective of the partnership was all about. Nevertheless, she decided not to linger around the place for fear of divine retribution and would hurry home.

Kasturi, her long lost friend, was sure to have attended Alice' funeral. She had no qualms about associating with the likes of Alice with whom she had a lot in common. Awra had always known that Kasturi lived by the seashore. She would make it part of her itinerary to wander around her house, which she had frequented as a girl. She would be keen on finding out for herself what it was that drove Kasturi to become a hobo as claimed by her kith.

The place looked the same as she had left it decades ago, with the four carved pillars supporting the stoop, the infamous yellow distemper on the walls, and the red baked Albuquerque and Sons tiles on the roof. The four coconut trees swayed along the flanks of the house. There were a couple of boats on the hot sand outside the house waiting to be fixed before the fishing season commenced.

What was different? Fleeting into the house, Awra was certain to notice that there were three more portraits added to the existing ones on the walls in the prayer room, the recent among them startling her out of her wits. The framed pictures were adorned with sandalwood garlands, turmeric paste and *kumkum*. She was sure to snoop around to figure out what the menfolk standing reverentially in a circle in the courtyard were up to. She would snap

out of her ghostlike daze with the *Gurikar* sprinkling
the holy Ganges on their bowed heads with a cluster
of *thulasi* leaves, not being spared from the drizzle
herself. Awra would be mystified by the ritual and
wonder what the flurry was all about.

Awra having ascertained that Kasturi's *Bada*
Uncle, fifteen years their junior, whose cradle the
two of them had rocked playfully as children, was
no more and she was likely to look out for his spirit.
She would be distracted by the presence of family
which had come from afar to pay homage to his
memory and invite the departed soul to join his
ancestors. *Bada* uncle was a hulk of a man, a dreaded
cop from Mumbai. On the thirteenth day after his
passing away, his spirit was being ushered into the
house with a ceremonious *Ulai Leppuna*. The ritual
was believed to aid a soul in finding repose back
among its people and give up wandering aimlessly
for fear of being lost for eternity. He was the tallest
of men that Awra had ever seen with thickset fingers
and bloody eyes. She was sure to envy the attention
he was being given with a feast set in his honour.
But none could touch the fare till his spirit signalled
acceptance of the service. The family would wait
until someone sighted a crow eating the choicest of
food which *Bada* uncle had savoured in his lifetime,
served on a banana leaf and placed in the courtyard
of the house.

Unable to contain her inherent curiosity, Awra
was bound to be part of the melee. She would
conclusively sense the overpowering presence of the

departed predecessors of Kasturi, eager to receive one of their own. Such an atmosphere would be conducive for Awra to be hailed by the Reverend in the company of her parents.

Would she then have the pluck that Teru showed to dodge them? Would she engage them in a banter and annoy them with a series of questions which would force them to leave her alone? Would she bring herself to twist the Reverend's sagging bottom or attempt a similar trick on him and then look sceptically at his attendant companions to claim the benefit of doubt? asked Chibby and Tabby taking turns.

I wouldn't be surprised if she asked her grandfather, as to why the two sisters of whom her mother was magnolia-white whereas her aunt Mary was ebony-black? A detail that was often debated in muffled tones among family, a matter that always distracted the inquisitorial Awra, chuckled Tabby with his mouth full of words like Awras.

Would Grandpa be perceptive enough to know that she wasn't making any insinuation, but only speaking her mind on something everyone teased her aunt about? Tabby continued.

If she sighted her mother she was likely to ask,

Tell me Mama how do you debone the sole fish to make cutlets? retorted Chibby to keep the discourse going, something no chef had ever attempted.

II

Salvation Channel

Awra hasn't grown up in all these years. She still has umpteen questions up her sleeve, and expects others to think and act for her.

An exasperating habit, her mother would allege and turn to her companion spirits for solace,

Tell me, will my daughter be ready ever for reconciliation to merit eternal reward?

Going by Teru's journey through the huddle of those clouds and the discernment which came with it, I wish Awra would stop asking questions, and be receptive to revelation instead, said a reflective Tabby.

And you tell me that Awra can't lobby in her new status and seek the support of Christian Mothers or the Senior Citizens Forum or her husband to come to her rescue and tell her how to go about redeeming her soul, added a fretful Chibby.

Tabby was doubtful if her husband who always gave her a volley of instructions for each situation would step back as expected and watch and wait for the awakening in Awra. Only then would she be able to stop the incessant chatter and start focussing on her mission.

Who better than those who have walked this path to endorse the universal truth? Unlike the earthly pilgrimage, the soul's journey is unescorted. No daughter, no spouse, no mentor can intervene. Every soul is solitary on this transmigration as was Teru's. Her soul forged its path, unravelled the mysteries of life and resolved its existential dilemma. In this truth lies the less known secret on how to ascend into that state of bliss and unite with the cosmos.

Teru exemplified this truth, didn't she? mumbled Tabby, not quite able to digest the gravity of all that he had just spoken.

Minutes later, he said more to himself,

It must be true then that unlike the moggies, mankind is endowed with the intrinsic wisdom to know that on the day of reckoning, it's through self-determination that the soul perceives life. Life as lived, life with all its strengths and foibles, life in its entirety. No more of the fisticuffs with god or man.

As Awra would work her way through redemption, no matter how long it took, the elderly dependent from the family would hover about to find out why it is that Awra had diluted his coffee and curry, the only things that pepped his life. So, would a series of her housemaids wanting to know why they didn't get to eat what they had cooked for the household when it was fresh, but when it almost went rancid. Maggie, one among them, still nursed a grouse and may be expected to talk back, as always.

Why did you spray me with cold water when all I wanted were a few extra winks of sleep? At that unearthly hour, too. I was only twelve then.

Agonized, angry, aggrieved, all of them had stagnated on the lowest and the bleakest of clouds.

Looking at Chibby's downcast face, Tabby went about consoling her,

Chibby, don't be disheartened. Even a hard-core empiricist will eventually learn to read the Life Spirit and respond to it.

Yet Tabby feared that Awra may not be perceptive to the anguish she had wrought upon her domestic staff and the dependent elder.

How I wish Awra would free herself from these fetters and not jeopardise her own redemption. If only the tormented would let bygones be bygones and help her attain *moksha,* I would be spared this agony cried Chibby.

C'mon Chibby, let this not take the wind out of your sail.

What next? Would Awra be able to break free from this snare that impedes her soul-purpose? Will the redeemed succeed in getting her to see the out-worldly truth in its purity, given their super-conscious progressive state? asked a troubled Chibby in response.

You are beginning to speak just like Awra teased Tabby. Too many questions make me breathless.

He didn't want to disappoint Chibby by placing before her the unvarnished truth that it was going to be an extra-arduous journey for Awra as it is for most of mankind.

Who can tell? It could take several lifetimes for Awra to accept and overcome her proclivity for self over others. Failing, she'd be desolated.

Getting Teru to concede and see another point of view was a gargantuan task, said Tabby who was well versed in the purgatorial passage to redemption of a being. Thanks to Teru for lessons so dear.

For if Awra didn't make the move, for so long will the fate of those in the loop be restricted to the lower clouds, decried Chibby with tears marking dark rivulets on her face. If there was anything to what Tabby professed, then she wanted Awra to go through the journey giving up her dalliance with this elusive life.

What if she brusquely said as always,

I'm just like this. I've told God that He cannot punish me. I've been fashioned to think, feel and act the way I do and I can't help the outcome, so, Chibby mimicked Awra.

Can't the Reverend ask Teru who had known her, to intercede for Awra? The Reverend still smarting from the sting might just about ask her to oblige, supposed Tabby.

Hardly had he thought of it, he remembered that there were no piggyback rides to *nirvana*.

Chibby was hopeful for Awra for outlandish reasons. Awra wouldn't be able to suffer the icy feel of the clouds with her woollens - her monkey cap, gloves and socks and shawls left behind in her black box; or withstand the darkness of the firmament in the company of those in a state of limbo, with the torch left behind under her pillow; or endure the fear of being raped and her throat slit by an unrepentant soul for no gain whatsoever, except to gratify lust. After all, she would be leaving behind her physical shell, her armour and there was only so much she would be able to do to protect herself. Her soul-force sitting on the fence couldn't be counted on at this critical juncture, not without atonement.

Could this push her to weigh other options, say reconciliation? asked Chibby.

Meandering through her yesterdays, Awra was sure to learn that it takes all kinds of people and experience to live life and understand the soul-purpose behind it. If Awra immersed herself in the new mediation, she is certain to see her child maid Maggie sitting aloft a cloud clutching her griping stomach. All for having eaten the near odorous *kanji* served to her day after day. If Awra could see the causal link for the distress, Maggie would be relieved and Awra would move up by a few notches, thought Tabby. One little move on Awra's part, a grain of remorse was all that was needed to set the reckoning rolling for everyone in her loop, contemplated the two felines.

But would she relent? asked both Tabby and Chibby at once.

If only Awra looked at *Dattu* in the eye, she would see tears rolling down his cheeks, for the disdain she had shown his orphaned children after he was gone. There was going to be no redemption for any of them, not unless Awra sought the liberation of her soul, of her own volition.

Tabby and Chibby had their reservation on the matter.

It was not given to them to know what turn Awra's journey would take after she ceased to exist. It was good to see Awra live a life that she cherished immensely. If she were to die, she is sure to miss the creature comforts of this world to which she was attached to like the Siamese twins. If she were to move on, she would be required to look back at her life, however entangled it might have been, and introspect. But for Awra, death was merely an eventuality and an end all. Accountability, reckoning and judgement, were for the courts of the living. Once dead, nothing mattered.

If it were to the contrary, does it mean she'd be stuck on those bleak clouds, asked Chibby incredulously.

When she does make the time to contemplate, in days after she is gone, or maybe eons from now, her compulsive curiosity is likely to catapult her to the unforeseen realization of a sublime life on the other side, stated Tabby solemnly.

Do you think I will be permitted to tag along?

Chibby, if you seek my counsel, we are better off here. When Awra's time ends, her todays will merge with all her yesterdays and the life to come. Let us leave the dead to the Reverend and his legions. Let the living deal with life.

What am I to tell Awra if she were to ask me, why it is that cats are blessed with nine lives and not mankind?

Tabby with misty eyes told her what Teru always professed,

One lifetime is a blessing if it's free from bondage. Such a life is worth nine times nine.

EPILOGUE

All sorrows can be borne if you put them in a story or tell a story about them.

Isak Terkel

Sitting by the window, I have been watching a pair of Brahminy kites hog the view of the valley outside. It is filled with ten thousand or more swaying coconut palms, intercepted by sporadic red tile-roofed houses. I have seen them live their lives with zen like serenity, epitomising *amor fati.* They face the sun and the rain, the storm and the calm without getting their wings ruffled, such that they could go on living life which is their lot, in all its details, over and over, for infinity.

Unlike Teru who resisted adversity and Awra who questioned the fundamental issues of life, to the kites life is invariable, season after season, life as fate has ordained. Their story is configured, and the kites seem not to be hassled about it.

For Teru, her chronicle from birth to death is crowded with conflicts, and from death to her destination is wrought with bedlam. It runs in a thousand directions, crisscrossing between the familiar and the strange, amounting to an abstract text far from coherent. Teru is no 'amor fati'. She challenges the world order by returning from death to life as against moving from life to death. She leaves us in doubt of her ever becoming one with the cosmic directive. Awra on the other hand, is a radical who questions the very existence of god, heaven and hell. Their story as a result appears flawed. Yet it holds its own as the tension in the journey evolves to find its way out of life's scuffles.

In the end, the journey, from life to death and from death to cloud nine, turns out to be conceivable for Teru and probable for Awra. It's not going to be a fairy tale ending for either of them. Given Teru's nature and circumstances, she would have to return to life to make sense of it. Whereas for Awra, she is seen rationalising and at times attempting to reorder life to have it her way. We can only presume that she too will revisit life and rewrite her script to move on to be one with the universe.

To accomplish this objective, both must sift through an assortment of people, experiences, places and beliefs, not all of them homogenous. We see diverse communities at odds with each other through the centuries impacting the lives of these two women. The native Kodavas fought the Sultan to preserve their ethnic identity and race; the Kurubas resisted their landlord, even if for one day in the year, questioning their enslavement in the guise of Kunde Festival; the Mappilas constrained to be Muslims preferred to keep a low profile despite having a common ancestry with the Kodavas and the Christians as a later *entrée* to the arena did much the same. Subsequently, the narrative becomes an amalgam of varied thoughts and ideas, cultures and communities, incohesive at times.

History placed Teru's ancestors among the Kodavas. The Kodavas as chronicled are a distinct community. For centuries, they have lived in Kodagu cultivating paddy fields, raising cattle herds and carrying arms during war. Except bearing arms, Teru's ancestors immersed themselves in the occupation, culture and interests of the mainstream Kodavas, sustaining their own faith, language and home-grown practices.

Theories abound as to the origin of the Kodavas. It is said that they could be the native inhabitants of the region or the descendants of the broad-headed stock who entered the Indus Valley during the Mohenjo-Daro period before the arrival of the Indo-Aryans. Eventually, they migrated to Kodagu *(Hutton, as quoted by Balakrishnan in 1976)*. Another view is that the Kodavas are the descendants of Scythians *(Connor 1870, Rice 1878)*. One other substantiates the fact that the ancestors of the Kodavas were either pre-Muslim Kurds or pre-Christian Caucasians *(Lt. Col. K. C. Ponnappa's A Study of the Origins of Coorgs)*. The *Kaveri Purana* claims that Chandra Varma, a Kshatriya warrior, was the ancestor of this 'fierce' race of the Kodavas. During his pilgrimage, to several holy places to the South of India, he came into Kodagu. He found that the banks of River Kaveri was a fertile uninhabited jungle land. He settled there with his men and prospered. Chandra Varma became the first Raja of the Coorg principality and his descendants came to be called the Kodava race.

Teru, born and raised among the Kodavas, embraced the land of her birth with a slight apprehension and yet accepted every deity and myth that was part of its matrix, as her own. The ordeals of their gods and men, became her ordeals as well. Teru's account of the tribulations of the Thamme of Pannagala becomes stirring as a result. 'Teru Lived' among such a people and her vestiges have now become one with the land that welcomed her forefathers, who found refuge in Kodagu under Dodda Veerarajendra. The fifteen years of imprisonment of her ancestors under Tipu at Seringapatam changed the course of history for Teru, uprooting her folks from the land of her forefathers, which is Kodial or the present-day Canara.

The captivity and imprisonment of 60,000 to 80,000 Mangalorean Catholics at Seringapatam (1784–1799) by Tipu Sultan, the de facto ruler of the Kingdom of Mysore, was a wretched period for Teru's community. Though it is said to have happened because of political rather than religious compulsions, the community took the bashing. To this day, the estranged descendants writhe from nostalgia for a return home, with a yearning for acceptance by the parent community. The linguistic, cultural, social and occupational drift between them has grown into a chasm over the centuries which is hard to wish away. The sense of being treated as a pariah rankles among those who paid the price on behalf of the community. This is replicated in the squabble between Teru's parents, with the caste superior *bamonn* spouse accusing the other of being a *sudra*. The ramifications of the gulf between the two, the home of her ancestors and the home she has embraced, make Teru and her soul traverse between Kodagu and Kodial and Kodial and Kodagu, not quite belonging anywhere.

Teru's life is a tousled one. Yet, in life as in death, Teru is at home with the Kodava Mappila such as Aaleema and her father. She is a part of the whole. Teru couldn't escape the camaraderie between them as they constitute a sizable chunk of the population of Kodagu. They are the Muslim descendants of Kodavas who were forcibly converted to Islam by Tipu over his repeated forays into Kodagu and his subsequent capture and imprisonment and conversion of them at Seringapatam in the 18th century. After Tipu's fall, they went back home, but a return to their original faith remained an illusion as once converted to Islam, the Kodavas refused to reinitiate them to the faith of their forefathers. However, they continue to maintain their original Kodava clan names, dress habits and Kodava mother tongue.

To Teru, the Mappilas are as much the children of the soil as she is and they become a parcel of her saga as well. Consequently, her salvation is not plausible without Alira Mammunchi Maestry's manoeuvrings in the cloud-laden firmament leading to the imposing Spirit Pageant.

On the lower-end of the spectrum is the Kuruba, of the Yadava lineage mentioned in the *Puranas*. He doesn't fail to garner Teru's attention. To her, they were like the biblical shepherds whose traditional occupation was shepherding and hunting. She saw them regularly walking down the meandering dykes among the fields of paddy to go into town for a cup of that delectable *"chai"* at Ummer Kaka's. Their Kunde Festival was an integral part of her life. To her, it was enough to know that like her, they were human, flesh and blood, with rage and romance in their hearts, especially in the context of Seethe's ordeal. It didn't matter to her that most South Indian dynasties from the Pallavas to the Yadurayas were pastoralist and cowherd groups who belonged to the Kuruba lineage (*Ramachandra Chintaman Dhere, a scholar of the religious traditions of Maharashtra*).

Awra is spared from being swept into the vortex of having to live in so convoluted a society. Her only cross is poverty which she carried with *amor fati*. Her interactions with the communities around her were limited to her own kind. The major exceptions were the Adhikaris, whom she unwittingly harassed for a while with her passion for breeding fish.

The fisherfolk with whom her rapport was limited to haggling deals over the price of fish reflect the restricted life that she lived. This is inclusive of her amicable ties with Kasturi, a Mogaveera.

The Mogaveera community lives in the costal belt of Karnataka in India and is predominantly known for fishing and other maritime activities. Awra was in awe of their incredible religious and social practices. On her supposed after life jaunt, she is sure to be intrigued by their worship of Panjurli, a wild boar deity. It is supposed that he was brought to the earth by Shiva as a divine spirit to protect and uplift the masses from evil to good. At Kasturi's house by the sea, out of sheer curiosity, Awra's spirit is certain to sneak into the miniature temple, with room enough for no more than one, dedicated to this boar deity who resembled Prince Gooty. Walking into Kasturi's house, she would find that Panjurli's sister Kallurti too had a place of honour on an ornamental swing at the altar of a pantheon of gods. Awra's soul-spirit would wait for an opportunity to rock the swing when no one was paying attention.

But what would surely agitate Awra was the small outhouse where she had seen a perturbed Kasturi spending three days in the month, as an adolescent, all alone. In a room that was accommodating enough to house an average sized individual who could just about stand and stretch herself without running into the walls. This was the fate of the other women in the family as well, with a dog in a makeshift kennel and a batch of hens in a coop on either side of the midget- house for company. Awra's sway with the rest of the folks beyond her home and neighbourhood was minimalistic as is the life of folks in a city.

At the end of the day, whether one is from a village or a city, the journey through life and death is common to all and sundry as delineated by the folks in the tale. The soul ultimately returns to its source. The only distinction being, the journey is personalised by the itinerant by his acceptance or rejection of his experiences, upon which depends the emancipation of the soul. Manjula's husband's disintegration is an anomaly, but not without hope should he resolve the scuffle with his soul. Teru conquers her shortcomings with stoicism when it mattered most and it is expected of Awra to do the same when the clock begins to tick for her.

The Brahminy kites, I see them now gliding, now wheeling and coasting by turns, diving pronto over a prey, presently soaring as if to escort souls on their way to where the others before them have careened to. They make no distinction between the Kuruba, the Kodava, the Mappila, the Canara or the Kodava Catholic, the Mogaveera, the brahman and Teru and Awra. To them each is a part of the whole and the whole of which each is a part. Together, providence has roiled them to form the mystic knot of Brahma.

End

ACKNOWLEDGEMENT

I was fascinated with the lives of Maria Augusta Trapp and her family, ever since the movie *The Sound of Music*. Continuing to delve into their lives, I chanced upon Maria's account of her visit to a chapel on the wooded slopes of a picturesque valley in Tyrol. There, she had playfully taken the dangling rope to try out the sound of the bell. Doing so, she told her writer friend, 'I wish I could become a writer too, …' She had no idea at that time, that if someone rang the bell while pronouncing a wish, it would come true, provided the person was not aware of the legend. For, this was no ordinary but a wishing bell. It is believed that anyone ringing the bell once in a hundred years or so, is in for a wish fulfilment. Maria wrote *The Story of the Trapp Family Singers*, depicting their travails and escape from the war-weary Austria to freedom, soon after.

If a visit to the chapel at Tyrol is all it takes to become a writer, then I am in. Who can tell, with the wish fulfillment, anyone can wax lucky and pen a story. I believe that there is in each one of us an untold story waiting to be told.

For now, let me peal the chime on my door and get your attention to the tale I wish to share with you.

Let me begin by acknowledging the several people, institutions and sources who churned my thoughts and experiences leading to that yarn.

I owe more than gratitude to my parents for my upbringing despite their difficult circumstances and the freedom they gave their girl child to think freely and live nobly.

To all my siblings, without whose unsolicited and critical acclaim half my battles would have remained un-fought and my character un-evolved. Thanks to all seven of them for never ceasing to raise the bar and daring me to do one notch better.

I cross my heart and say a prayer for the repose of the souls of my forebears whose presence I have evoked in my narration; for empowering me to straddle my heritage through generations to the present, for working in close liaison with the living to make life and death acceptable to me.

To a host of my friends for letting me use some of their insights and stories about mothers and grandmothers; for their religious and cultural take on life and death; for their encouragement and support in helping me give shape to a story and transform it from an admixture of chaos to a comprehensible tale. Thank you.

- to Shruti P. Bhandary, my light house, who kept me on the course whenever I hit the rock and anything hard
- to a young mind in Vidya Shenoy, for scanning my script with a fine-tooth comb for factual, cultural, historical and literary representations and for helping me believe in myself
- to Dr. Geralyn Pinto, for being my inspiration
- to Dr. Urmila Shetty for her support in helping me complete the project
- to Dr. Malini Hebbar for editing the text
- to Ms. Flossy Mendonca and Mr. Clifford W De Silva for filling me in on the many Konkani terms to help me capture their essence
- to the Apostolic Carmel sisters with whom I spent the best part of my life, for moulding my attitude, character and values, for helping me find my voice, a myriad *namaskars*
- to Toastmasters International, an organization which provides a platform to hone communication and leadership skills, for letting me explore my potential as a story teller
- and to everyone who helped me surprise myself

I have heard it said, that the world can no longer come up with an unprecedented idea. Perhaps there is a grain of truth in this notion. Nevertheless, I would like to acknowledge certain words, phrases, concepts, stories and episodes that I have either taken from other writers and sources partially or fully. Often, some of them have coloured my language, style, interpretation and situation. My reference to cats in action, I owe to Robert Fulghum's *All I Really Need to Know I Learned in Kindergarten,* where he talks about racoons on heat. The episode of raccoon pair mating in the cellar, underneath his bed room year after year, with a lot of violence rather than romance, demystifies the attention love receives. Their attributes are seen in Tabby and Chibby whenever they screech and scratch.

To Abraham Verghese' *Cutting for Stone,* a book I kept returning to while coursing through my own journey as a writer, to him I owe my use of the concept of 'heurism,' in which Awra indulges. Life is full of them. To her an orange sky meant a big catch of pink perch and a deathly stillness among trees was a sure sign of a looming storm or a tsunami. So too, Verghese' stance on how to die as much as how to live life, with a characteristic openness and simplicity which enabled me to accept life and death with equanimity.

As a netizen, I couldn't have done what I have done without surfing for info and drawing inspiration from quotes on life and death. I have visited, *www. StevePavlina.rip* and been influenced by articles and lectures on 'Life After Death' and 'Personal Development for Dead People.' 'The Grail Message' and 'Deposited This Life!' which have helped me grapple with the idea of death. The line, 'I suppose my daughter has gone on a date with death,' is a modified line taken from a quote on death, and the source eludes me for some reason. My apologies for the lapse. The phrase – 'amplified high fidelity razor sharp clinks,' surfaced like a wave, to aptly capture the sounds made by the rattling sounds of breaking of glass and bone-china crockery. I'm afraid, it has its source in some advertisement for high resonant musical applications. I could be wrong.

The phrase 'thorn birds' flew straight out of Colleen McCullough's *The Thorn Birds* to depict the sexual foibles between the young and the celibate, not so uncommon, though seldom acknowledged.

The several dreams that punctuate the narration to present death or out of body experiences, seemingly vicarious, bring out yet another facet of death. The stuff that dreams are made of baffle the living and for these hair-raising dream experiences I'm grateful to Vima, my sister-in-law. Thank you for letting me use them from your repertoire of dreams.

The reader will recognize the term, 'endian' used in a literal context. Jonathan Swift in his *Gulliver's Travels* uses it to describe the conflict between two political factions who fight over the right way of breaking an egg - small end or the big end? Such of them were called big 'endians' or small 'endians' depending on the side they belonged to. In the context of this tale, it refers to the one placed last in the scheme of things.

The letter to Queen Bess is made up. However, the historical aspects of her character are authentic. So too the fact, that a long time ago, a fellowman from my community dashed off a proposal of marriage to an incumbent princess.

'His Master's Voice', the unofficial name of a large British record label with Nipper listening to a wind-up gramophone is etched into the psyche of those who grew up owning a gramophone. The line having been in the public domain for so long, I guess one is free to use it as one chooses to. All the same, thanks to Nipper for inspiring the slogan.

To my family: Gerard, Majella, Kishore and Shawn who kept looking at me suspiciously as I went tap tap on the keyboard day in and day out, thanks for not butting into my personal space. My precious Grandchildren Ben and Dan, you were my Muse, my fire of creativity, I couldn't let you down ever. For you, I would never let my spirit flag. Bless you.

There could be those well-wishers, sources and people I may have overlooked mentioning. The slip is not intentional. I am convinced that the many personal and professional encounters in life impact and leave indelible imprints on our minds. So too, the unwritten script, your own experiences and interpretation of death, are sure to be most interesting. You are my sustenance and fulfilment. I count on you for luck and inspiration.

Loads and loads of gratitude to my Mother and my Mother-in-law out of whom the two women emerged. That is where the similarities end as the rest is mere fiction and fantasy. Any resemblance thereof to the two matriarchs and folks in their circle remote or otherwise is accidental.

Ago tibi maximus gratias ago.
Enjoy the story.

FOOT NOTES

a:

aab - grandfather in Konkani language

aan - father

abolim - a yellow or peach coloured flower strung together and used to adorn the coiffed hair of a Konkani speaking catholic bride in India, *crossandra infundibuliformis*

ad nauseam - is a Latin term for argument or other discussion that has continued 'to [the point of] nausea'

adolo - a curved knife fixed on a long stool for cutting fish and meat seated on it, in Konkani, a language spoken predominantly in South Kanara and Goa

Agnessa, ootgo.

Ootgo Agnessa - Agnessa is an indigenous version for Agnes, in Konkani language. The statement means 'Wake up girl, wake up'

aimara - a parapet with a timber top adorning the front veranda of the house, in Kodava language

Aiyappa - is a Hindu deity worshiped in temples in South India

aiyya - master in Malayalam, a language commonly spoken in Kerala

Birbal's twice

bitten cat - refers to the story of Birbal's cat which was trained by him to stay away from milk by having it dip its mouth in scalding hot milk, attributing to the saying, once bitten twice shy

akhai - paternal aunt in Konkani language, also tintin (pronounced thee-theen)

Ambla Pole - The confluence of 2 mountain rivers in Kodagu, known as 'Ambla Pole'. It is believed that the 'Rain god' Igguthappa with his brothers and sister had lunch on the banks of this river

amor fati - is a Latin phrase meaning "love of one's fate". It is used to describe an attitude characterized by an acceptance of the events or situations that occur in one's life

anna - a currency unit formerly used in India and Pakistan, equal to 1/16 of a rupee

b:

bada - big in Hindi

bafaath - a red curry powder prepared with Indian condiments and spices, used to cook pork and other meats

bai - sister in Konkani language

baksheesh - gratuity, tip given for the service rendered

bale enna

Krishna - come my Krishna, in Tulu, a language spoken by people of South Kanara. Krishna is the god of compassion, tenderness and love in Hinduism

Bamonn/

Brahman - A Brahman is a member of the highest Hindu caste, originally that of priesthood. The descendants of Konkani speaking Brahmin converts to Roman Catholicism are known as Bamonns. It's a caste among the Goan and Mangalorean Catholics

bappu - paternal uncle, in Konkani

batti - unit of measurement, equivalent to 48 kilograms, used in Kodagu

bayamma - a catholic matronly figure in Mangalore

bebdo - a drunk, in Konkani

beedi - tobacco rolled in *Kendu* or *Kachnar* leaves for smoking

Benda Kaalu Ooru - meaning 'town of boiled beans,' is based on a tale of King Veera Ballala II of the Hoysala dynasty in 1120 AD who was fed boiled beans by an old woman in the forest. Another theory is that the name 'Bengalooru' was recorded much before King Ballala's time in a 9th century inscription found in a temple in Begur village near Bangalore

Bethel - a place that is regarded as sacred or holy, also a chapel for sailors and other seafarers. In this instance, it refers to Awra's aunt's house overlooking the sea

Bhagavathi - Bhagavathi is a popular deity in the Indian states of Kerala, Karnataka, Goa and Konkan

biriyani - flavoured basmati rice cooked with spices, meat/ vegetables

boondhi

laddoos - laddoos are ball-shaped sweets popular in the Indian Subcontinent. Laddoos are made of flour, mixed dough and sugar with other ingredients that vary by recipe

c:

carpe diem - to seize the day

chaddies - inner wear made of striped cloth, used by rural men

chai - tea in most Indian languages

chakli - an Indian savoury made of rice and urad dhal, deep fried in oil

champaks - ivory coloured flowers known for their fragrance, *magnolia champaca*

Chamundi - goddess of war and pestilence and other disasters. She is the Hindu Divine Mother

Chanel - perfume of the legendary Chanel-House, a branded perfume of long standing

Chembu - a small brass or copper pot to carry water

Chickpet - chikka-small, pete-town- small town, in Virajpet to the south of Coorg

Chingaari - the adorned one, also used as a proper noun, in Malayalam, Kodava and Kannada languages

chingiri ari - slender fine rice, with a gentle aroma, used in the preparation of pilaff and biriyani

chor - rogue/thief in Hindi

chorizo - spiced pork sausages in Spanish

chunam - limestone paste

copra - desiccated coconut chips

croande - croaking frog version of the Kuruba's *Kunde Kunde*

d:

Daijiworld - Mangalore based News Media portal

Dattu – an older brother, in Konkani language

Deccan Herald - English daily newspaper of Karnataka since 1948

Devara Kadu - These are sacred groves, most of which are communally protected. Kodavas have maintained some thousand Devara Kadu's dedicated to Aiyappan, the forest god

Devraj Urs

Market - Devaraja Urs was the erstwhile reformist Chief Minister of Karnataka. The commercial street in the city of Mysore and the market are named after him

Dharma

sado - a sari gifted to the bride by her mother in which she is dressed on her return to her husband's house at the end of the 'Home Coming' ceremony

Dhobi - washer man in Hindi

Diwali - festival of lights celebrated all over India in the month of November

Dodda Veerarajendra - Dodda Veerarajendra adorned the throne of Kodagu from 1791 to 1809 and is considered the hero of Haleri dynasty that ruled the land for more than 200 years

dokebaaz - a cheat in Hindi

Domus Aurea - aurum- gold, domum- house – 'house of gold' in Latin

donghi - cheat

doresaani - a white woman, an English lady in Kannada, a South Indian language

dovlo - a ladle made with coconut shell having a bamboo stick handle, in Konkani language

dukor - pig in Konkani

Dussehra - Vijayadashami celebration that is observed by Hindus to celebrate the victory of Lord Rama over Ravana, and of Durga over demons, like Mahishasura

e:

Engelberg - a place of scenic beauty in Switzerland

f:

FB - Face Book, a Social Networking Service

Fenny - sometimes spelt feni, is a spirit produced exclusively in Goa, India. There are two types of feni; cashew feni and toddy palm feni, depending on the original ingredient used

g:

ghol chillies - the spicy short and round red peppers grown in India

Gorga -rain cover made of palm leaves supported by splintered bamboo, to cover the head and the entire back, in Kannada, a language spoken in Karnataka, India. Also, known as Korambu in Tulu language

Grecian Urn - Keats in his poem 'Ode on a Grecian Urn' goes on to describe the pictures on the urn. The reference here is to a picture of a town emptied of its inhabitants. Consequently, the town is desolating and will forever be silent

G.R. - Georgius Rex, King George III of England, 1738-1820

Gurikar - head of a social, religious group responsible for religious and other ceremonies among Tulu speaking people of South Kanara

Guthu - any Bunt family name, symbolizing their matriarchal lineage

h:

hakoba - soft cotton fabric, popular and expensive for its fine hand-crafted embroidery all over the fabric

hara hara - commands given to the oxen pair at the plough share to move in the required direction

Harijans and

Girijans - a Harijan is a member of a hereditary Hindu group of the lowest social and ritual status; a Girijan is a member of the aboriginal peoples of India

Hebbale - is a small village in Somvarpet Taluk in Kodagu District famous for its view of river Cauvery

holeya - a Holeya is a member of a scheduled caste of India, Karnataka. In British India, Holeyas lived in Canara, Coorg Province and Mysore.

They were one of the lowest class, slaves who could be sold by the owner of the estate in which they were located

Reference- Sri Igguthappa Devaru- Evvamakka Debuvaru by Paradanda G. Chengappa, pg. 102 and Wikipedia

homa - is a ritual, wherein religious offerings are made to god through fire. Offerings include grains, clarified butter, milk, incense and grains

hooch - illicitly distilled alcoholic liquor

i:

idru - a heavy goblet of a medium size used to sip liquor from, in Konkani

imane - a huge house with a central courtyard belonging to a household with the same lineage, a place where their family deity is enshrined and worshipped, common among Kodavas

j:

Jayachamarajendra Wodeyar - He was the 25th and the last ruling Maharaja of the Kingdom of Mysore from 1940 to 1950. He was a noted philosopher, musicologist, political thinker, and philanthropist.

joy de vivre - exuberant enjoyment of life, in French

k:

Kabuliwalah - a trader from beyond the Pass in Kabul who sold silks and dry fruits in India. *Refer to R. Tagore's The Cabuliwallah*

kadi- patta - herb used to season the Indian curry, in Hindi, *Murraya Koenigii*

kaka - uncle in Malayalam

kanakadi - an ornamental silver stick with a scoop at one
end to extract ear-wax, worn by women on
their key chains, to the South of India

kanji - gruel or porridge made of rice, consumed as a
staple meal among the rural folks and often
served to the sick in South India

karma/karmic - sum of a person's actions in one of his
successive states of existence, viewed as
deciding his fate in the next birth

Karna - a central character in the Hindu epic *Mahabharata*.
Karna is often quoted for his sacrifice, courage,
charity, valor, and selflessness

kaththi - a crescent- shaped scythe with a curved blade,
with a wooden handle

kathri - Kathri in Kannada, a South Indian language,
stands for a pair of scissors. The crude kathri
birth was practiced by midwives in instances
of prolonged labour to exert pressure on the
peritoneum, to assist the mother in bearing
down the infant

Kerala - a state situated between the Arabian Sea to the
west and the Western Ghats to the east of India

Kismet - fate or karma

Kodava - a Kshatriya or a warrior clan living in Kodagu/
Coorg, located to the South of India

Kodial - refers to South Kanara, in Konkani, also spelt
Canara

Kodialbail - Kodialbail is a locality in the city of Mangalore
in Karnataka state of India. It is located 2 km to
the north of Hampankatta. It is home to some
of the most prestigious educational institutes
of Mangalore

Kolikata - meaning field of goddess Kali

kombu kottu, volaga - kombu is a crescent shaped, long
trumpet; kottu is the accompanying drum
peculiar to the Kodavas and the local culture. It

is also an oxymoron as the word is suggestive of the sound it produces; volaga- a high pitched trumpet played by the Kodavas on social occasions

koolies - a spectral spirit familiar to the Kodava tribe

kunde habba or the feast of the rumps - kunde is the butt, habba is a feast celebrated by the Kurubas in Kodagu

Reference: Karnatakada Janapada Acharanegalu by Dr. S. C. Ramesh, Publisher: Kannada Vishwavidyanilaya, Hampi

kunkum - a red dust used by Hindu women and sometimes men to make a round mark on the forehead, a religious symbol

kun'no khalear undeachi ruch-uch nam - one who has lived on husk or coarse food has no palate for bread which is gentle in taste, a saying in Konkani language

kuppasa - the traditional long coat worn by the Kodava men on important occasions

kuppayam - a loose full sleeved blouse worn by Mappila women folk in Kodagu and Kerala

kuruba - forest tribe in Karnataka

kuttumbolichcha - standing brass oil lamps in Kodava language; one such was gifted by Dodda Veerarajendra, the local king, to St. Ann's Church, Kodagu

Kyrie eleison - Lord have mercy in Latin

l:

laddoo - round confections made of rice, besan, rawa and sugar

light paarddh jethunda matha sari appundu - literally means turn on the lights and sleep, in Tulu language, South Kanara; metaphorically it

implies that if one has a tipple before going to
bed, one's illnesses will vanish

lladro - porcelain handmade figurines

lungi - a traditional length of cloth wrapped around the
body from waist down to the ankle as done in
Kerala and Tamil Nadu

m:

maama/ maam - maternal uncle in South Indian languages

machan- - platform erected on a tree to facilitate tiger
hunting; Hindi language

maestry - an overseer in South Indian languages

Maharaja - king

Mai - mother/grandmother in Konkani

Malabaris - residents of the district of Malabar in Kerala

Malayali - Dravidian people who live in the state of Kerala,
India

malcriado - a brat in Portuguese, pronounced as malchiriad
with a soft 'd' as in English 'this'

mantha sari appundu - all will be well, in Tulu language

mappila - a member of the largest Muslim group in
the Indian state of Kerala. Also refers to the
Kodavas who were converted forcibly to Islam
by Tipu

mea kulpa - have mercy in Latin

ménage à trois - a domestic arrangement in which three
people having romantic and/or sexual relations
with each other occupy the same household. It
is a form of polyamory

Mi Casa - 'My House' in Spanish

Mi Gasa - note the sound shift from Casa to Gasa as is
usually done by speakers of Malayalam

mishey - moustache in Kannada and Malayalam, South
Indian languages

mogrem - jasmines in Konkani

moksha -the transcendent state attained after being
     released from the cycle of rebirth

moong dhal
payasam - sweetened green gram porridge
mundappas - mangoes specific to Mangalore, plump and
     sweet
munde ganda – husband of a widow. The former word is a
     socially demeaning abuse used to downgrade
     widows
mundu - lungi worn by Malayalis, like the ones seen in
     Kerala and Tamil Nadu
murraha - forty-two seers of rice wrapped in straw, woven
     into a globular shape for transport and storage
Mylapore - a cultural hub and neighbourhood in the
     southern part of the city of Chennai

n:

naan thithillathe
kuul beppi, ninga
uppillathe
umbira? - I'll cook rice without fire; will you eat it without
     salt? In language spoken by Kodavas *(Reference-*
     B.S. Kushalappa, 1937, from 'Sri Igguthappa
     Devaru-Evvamakka Debuvaru' by Paradanda G.
     Chengappa, pg. 100)

neem - a tree of mahogany family *Meliaceae* known for its
     medicinal property, *Azadirachta indica*
nirvana -a transcendent state in which there is neither
     suffering, nor joy, neither desire, nor sense of
     self, and the subject is released from the effects
     of karma and the cycle of death and rebirth
nom de plume - a pseudonym used instead of one's real
     name

nouveau rich - refers to people who have only recently
        become rich and who have tastes and manners
        that others consider vulgar

p:

paan -betel leaf of ever green plant Piper Betle, chewed in
        the east with areca-nut parings

Padre - the title of a priest or chaplain in some countries

Pandi curry - pork curry in Kodava language

Pannangala - a pilgrimage centre frequented by the
        Kodavas to the South of Kodagu

pashmina -in Persian *pasm* means wool; under-fur of hairy
        quadrupeds in Tibet, especially that of goats as
        used for Cashmere shawls

pathalakolli - a deep bottomless gorge, as deep as hell

patioie - thick dough made of sweetened rice and jack
        fruit, wrapped in banana or teak wood leaves
        and steamed, pronounced 'paat- oh-yeh'. There
        are variations of the same

payasam - a popular Kerala dessert served on special
        occasions

pixe - insane folks, pronounced pische

Porbule, Akka,

Bayamma, inchi

ora bale, thule

encha undu, thaja

halwa da lekka. Jeeva

da meen. Bale Anna - A porbulu is a konkani speaking
        Christian landlord from Mangalore, often
        known for his wealth, and opulent lifestyle.
        Akka is sister. Bayamma is a Konkani speaking
        elderly lady. Anna is a brother. These are
        accosted by the fisherwoman to come and take
        a look at the fresh fish that is as good as halwa,
        a sweet. She also tells them that the fish is live-
        in Tulu language.

q:

qawwali - a form of Sufi devotional music in South Asia, popular in the Punjab and Sindh regions of Pakistan and parts of North India

Queen Bess - is Elizabeth I, 1533-1603, Queen of England

r:

raath ki raani - fragrant flowers which bloom in the night, also known as night queen, *cestrum nocturnum*

raitha - an Indian salad made of curd, tomato, onion and green chillies

Raja seat - a seat reserved for a king, with a vantage point, as the one in Madikeri. It offers a pleasant spectacle of refreshing layers of greenery, chain of high and low- rise-mountains attired with mist. The Kings of Kodagu watched the setting sun and spent time with their queens here. In the story, the term refers to a seat coveted by all

Rama - a major deity of Hinduism, husband of Sita

Rangoli - is a folk art from India wherein patterns are created on the floor in living rooms or outside the threshold using materials such as coloured rice, dry flour, and coloured sand or flower petals. It is usually done during Deepawali, Onam, Pongal and other Indian festivals

rani ganda - queen's husband

rasam - is a South Indian soup, traditionally prepared using tamarind juice as a base, with the addition of tomato, chilli, black pepper, cumin and other spices as seasoning

raspoori - a variety of mangoes known for their nectarine sweet pulp

Rebecca - the Biblical woman whose favouritism to her younger son Jacob wrought great sorrow- Genesis 25-27 *rostear podil'lo, …,*

potacho, …, hullkot, …,

chediecho, …, papi, …, maljauvno - rosto-road, *podil'lo* - fallen- a
vagabond fallen on the road; *potacho*- literally
it means, 'from the stomach', but strangely the
word is used to refer to a bastard; *hullkot*- a
person of no worth in Marathi, a language of
Maharashtra, in India; *chediecho*- son of a bitch;
papi- a sinner; *maljauvno*- bastards

rotis - flattened bread made of rice flour, pan fried

s:

saambaar - curry with mixed vegetables, popular among
South Indians

sado - a red bridal sari gifted by the groom to deck the
bride with after the nuptials among Konkani
speaking Catholics

salaam - Namaste in Hindi/Urdu

sannas - steamed rice bread

sarey - corrupt version of 'Sir' in Malayalam and Tamil

sathanache saal - also known as the devil's tree, the bark of
which is known for its bitterness and medicinal
property. Legend has it that devil's dwell on
this tree and one would have to try getting a
piece of its bark at midnight. The person doing
so, would have to be stark naked like the devil.
He'd have to chip off the bark with anything
but metal. *Alstonia Scholaris*

Seven brothers - Legend has it that in ancient times from
what is now Kerala arrived seven celestial
children. They were siblings. The first 3
brothers stayed back in Kanjirath village,
Kerala. The remaining three brothers with
their sister moved towards Kodagu. The
fourth brother Igguthappa took base at Malma,
Kodagu and a temple was built for him at

Paadinaad. The fifth brother moved to Paloor in Kodagu where a temple was built for him. Their sister Thangamma (Thamme) settled down in Ponnangala village, near Kakkabe, where a shrine was built for her. The last brother Pemmayya moved further south and moved into Waynad in Kerala

Shambu and Ramu - are the oxen pairs. Shambu is an auspicious name and is a very gentle form of Shiva. Ramu is named after God Rama

shikar - hunting in Hindi

shoio - steamed string appas or rice noodles

Sita - central female character of the Hindu epic Ramayana

soro - liquor, in Konkani

suar - swine in Hindi, a derogatory abuse

subji - vegetable curry

sudra - a member of the lowest of the four major castes in the traditional society in India, comprising priestly class, artisans, labourers, and menials; also spelt as sudir

sultan - noble title meaning 'strength', 'authority', or 'power' in Arabic

supari killers - men bought over to eliminate those they wish to have out of their way

surantt -drunkard

t:

taluka - administrative district comprising of several villages for taxation purpose

tamales - In Mexico, tamales are made with dough from nixtamalized corn (hominy), called masa, and lard or vegetable shortening. Tamales are generally wrapped in corn husks or plantain leaves and steamed

tamasha - fuss or commotion in Hindi

tantric (N) - a person indulging in the ritual act of body and speech and mind

tawa - a frying pan in Hindi

tem - that, those, she

the Terracotta Army - soldiers and horse funerary terracotta statues depicting the armies of Qin Shi Huang, the first Emperor of China. It is a form of funerary art buried with the emperor in 210–209 BCE, whose purpose was to protect the emperor in his afterlife

thaja halwa lekka - like genuine halwa, a soft wheat/banana sweet cooked in ghee

thamdi bajjie - red amaranth, herb used as a vegetable; *Amaranthus Cruentus*

thamme - mother in Kodava language, another name for Thangamma, sister of Igguthappa

Thomas - one of the twelve apostles of Jesus. He is formally known as doubting Thomas as he doubted the resurrection of Jesus when he first learnt about it. John 20:24-28

Thorth - a thin towel used by a lady to cover her modesty over the blouse in Kerala: also used as a regular towel

thule encha undu - look, how good it is

Tipu - Tipu Sultan, 1750 –1799 known as the Tiger of Mysore, and was a ruler of the Kingdom of Mysore

tulasi - is a plant known from ancient times for its medicinal uses, *Ocimum tenuiflorum*

u:

ulai leppuna - ushering in

uuusss - fart in Kannada, language spoken in Karnataka

v:

vaddo - a ward or division, like an avenue to facilitate administration

vakhil baank - long, no nonsense bench with backrest and arms, used at a lawyer's office, also treasured in traditional households and sought after by connoisseurs of antique furniture

vermicelli payasam - vermicelli is pasta made in long slender threads. Kheer or payasam is a South Asian pudding made by cooking vermicelli in milk and sugar

vindaloo - spicy Goan masala paste used as the base in pork and chicken curry

w:

Warli figures - cultural and intellectual property of the tribe or Adivasis living in the areas of Maharashtra - Gujarat. The art figures are indigenous to the tribe

Wild Jack - a tree with miniature jackfruit like fruits, *Anjili Chakka, atrocarpus hirsutus*

End